THE LOVE TRAP

"There is only one way we can save ourselves," the Duke said, "although I am almost afraid to suggest it to you."

"If I can save you . . . and myself . . . I will do anything . . . anything!"

Janeta gave a little shudder which seemed to shake her whole body before she added:

"How could I marry a man like him, and not go mad with the horror of it? How could you marry her and hurt all those who believe in you?"

"Exactly," the Duke said, "and therefore we have to take what may seem to you a rather drastic step."

There was a little pause before Janeta said in a very small voice:

"What do we have to do?"

A Camfield Novel of Love
by Barbara Cartland

_____

"Barbara Cartland's novels are all distinguished by their intelligence, good sense, and good nature . . ."

—ROMANTIC TIMES

"Who could give better advice on how to keep your romance going strong than the world's most famous romance novelist, Barbara Cartland?"

—THE STAR

CAMFIELD NOVELS OF LOVE
by *Barbara Cartland*

Other books by *Barbara Cartland*

Camfield Place,
Hatfield
Hertfordshire,
England

Dearest Reader,

Camfield Novels of Love mark a very exciting era of my books with Jove. They have already published nearly two hundred of my titles since they became my first publisher in America, and now all my original paperback romances in the future will be published exclusively by them.

As you already know, Camfield Place in Hertfordshire is my home, which originally existed in 1275, but was rebuilt in 1867 by the grandfather of Beatrix Potter.

It was here in this lovely house, with the best view in the county, that she wrote *The Tale of Peter Rabbit*. Mr. McGregor's garden is exactly as she described it. The door in the wall that the fat little rabbit could not squeeze underneath and the goldfish pool where the white cat sat twitching its tail are still there.

I had Camfield Place blessed when I came here in 1950 and was so happy with my husband until he died, and now with my children and grandchildren, that I know the atmosphere is filled with love and we have all been very lucky.

It is easy here to write of love and I know you will enjoy the Camfield Novels of Love. Their plots are definitely exciting and the covers very romantic. They come to you, like all my books, with love.

Bless you,

A NEW CAMFIELD NOVEL OF LOVE BY

BARBARA CARTLAND

The Love Trap

A JOVE BOOK

THE LOVE TRAP

A Jove Book / published by arrangement with
the author

PRINTING HISTORY
Jove edition/October 1986

ISBN: 0-515-08714-9

Jove Books are published by The Berkley Publishing Group,
200 Madison Avenue, New York, N.Y. 10016.
The words "A JOVE BOOK" and the "J" with sunburst
are trademarks belonging to Jove Publications, Inc.

PRINTED IN THE UNITED STATES OF AMERICA

AUTHOR'S NOTE

BELLADONNA is one of the oldest poisons in herbal history. At the same time, in the homeopathic form it can be a valuable medicine, and minute quantities of a tincture made from the berries of the Belladonna will act as the prophylactic against scarlet fever.

Yet Belladonna is dangerous and the botanical name Atropa connects it mythologically with one of the Fates, to whom were entrusted the shears with which to cut the thread of human life.

Deadly Nightshade, as Belladonna is more often called in England, should never be grown in a garden where there are children, as they are tempted to taste the attractive, brightly coloured berries.

Doctor Fernie says that one of the peculiarities of poisoning caused by this berry is complete loss of voice, a curious movement of the hands and fingers, and a bending backwards and forwards of the body. It affects specifically the brain and the bladder, and influences all cold extremities and all forms of illusions of sight.

chapter one

1870

THE Duke of Wynchester felt he was falling asleep and knew it was time he left.

It was not surprising, since his love-making with the woman now lying beside him had been passionate and insatiable since the early hours of the evening, when they had come to bed.

In all his numerous love-affairs, and there had been a great number of them, the Duke had never found anyone quite so passionate or so demanding as Olive Brandon.

The Duke was very fastidious in the choice of those on whom he bestowed his favours, and although when he first saw Lady Brandon he had thought she was without exception the most beautiful woman he had ever seen, she had not attracted him to the point where he felt he must become involved with her.

But Olive Brandon had had very different ideas.

The Duke was the best-looking, the wealthiest, and the most important man at Court, and she determined, with an iron will which had grown stronger than steel in the last few years, that she would have him.

Olive had developed her determination long before she astounded London with her beauty.

She had realised when she was quite young how valuable her looks could be to her. When she was brought to London for a Season by her father and mother who lived in the depths of Gloucestershire, she had known that she must make the best of the two months she would have before they returned to the country, as it was unlikely she would ever have such a chance again.

Her father was a fox-hunting Squire who was very popular in his own County, but was quite unknown in the fashionable circles in which Olive longed to move.

Her mother had aristocratic connections, but most of them had daughters of their own and would not be inclined to put themselves out for another débutante.

Olive had a flair for making herself noticed in an almost theatrical manner, and she cajoled, pleaded, and insisted on her mother buying the gowns she wanted.

She knew that when she walked into a Ball-Room, she would cause a sensation.

Nevertheless, it required a great deal of persistence and cunning to ensnare a comparatively distinguished husband in her first Season.

Lord Brandon was a widower of over fifty, but with Olive's huge eyes hypnotising him, he had fallen in love as if he were a boy of twenty.

Olive had married just as she had planned, with a well-publicised ceremony at St. George's Hanover Square, and a crowded Reception in Lord Brandon's house in Park Lane.

From that moment she entered the world she had dreamed about and had longed to be part of.

She was clever enough not to arouse in her husband the least suspicion when she took lovers, and this was not very difficult as he grew older and liked to spend much of his time fishing and racing.

Fishing often took him to the far north of Scotland, which meant he was conveniently out of the way, while racing was to Olive an extremely boring pastime, unless she could show herself off at Ascot or Goodwood in a fashionable house-party.

Everything worked out extremely well, and Lord Brandon, although he was not as ardent as he had been when they first married, was still in love with his wife, when she saw the Duke of Wynchester.

It had been impossible for her not to notice him, for he stood head and shoulders above the other men in the Throne Room at Buckingham Palace, and wearing his decorations, looked to Olive's eyes exactly as if he had stepped out from one of the stories she had told herself when as Cinderella she met Prince Charming.

The Duke, however, was at first very elusive.

He was not only continuously in demand by the Prince of Wales at Marlborough House, to which she was not invited, but he spent a great deal of time watching the training of his horses on which he raced and hunted.

Precisely because he was single, he was inevitably the favourite of every hostess, and, of course, of every ambitious Mama, who thought wistfully that by some earth-shattering luck he might look at one of her offspring.

In fact, the Duke at thirty-three was determined still to keep his freedom.

In the high Society in which he moved it was taken for granted that a woman after some years of marriage, having presented her husband with an heir and perhaps two or three other children, should amuse herself in the same way as he had always been able to do, without there being too much fuss about it.

The unfortunate thing, however, was that Olive did not qualify for this category because, although it was something Lord Brandon longed for, she had not given him an heir.

This did not so much worry her, since she did not like children and had no wish to spoil the perfection of her figure.

At the same time, she was well aware that it was what was expected of her and that although he never said so in so many words, her husband was disappointed.

She knew that George Brandon was fanatically proud besides being exceedingly jealous, and should he suspect that she was being in any way unfaithful to him, he would undoubtedly vent his wrath on her as well as on any man who had seduced her.

She was delighted when, although it was only the beginning of June, George had an invitation to fish on the River Tay in Scotland, which he found very tempting.

"Of course you must go, dearest," she said. "It is very kind of the Earl to ask you, and as it is a river you have never fished before, you must accept."

"I would like to go," Lord Brandon admitted. "At the same time, I do not like to leave you alone in London."

Olive had laughed that silvery sound which was like a peal of bells.

"I shall be perfectly all right," she said. "And you know, dearest George, how much you hate those large dinner-parties night after night, which usually give you indigestion."

This was true, and Lord Brandon needed little more persuasion to accept the Earl of Kilkenay's invitation.

When he left for Scotland, Olive's heart leapt.

This was exactly what she had been waiting for. For the last three months she had been enticing, beguiling, and in her own way mesmerising the Duke, until he found it almost impossible to resist her.

The evening after her husband had left she asked him to dinner at her house, but was clever enough to invite other guests also.

This was not what he had expected, and he was quite surprised when he found there were two other couples, both of whom he knew, the men in particular being close friends.

They had laughed a great deal, enjoying the excellent food and wine, which Olive took great care always to provide for her guests. Then when the others had left at a quite reasonable hour, Olive had looked at the Duke questioningly.

She was looking exceedingly lovely in a gown with a bustle of green tulle, which matched the green of her eyes and the emeralds in her dark hair.

A necklace of the same stones accentuated the perfection of her magnolia skin, which the Duke thought was whiter than any other woman's he had ever seen.

For a moment he told himself that while she was very lovely, the climax to the evening was too obviously planned, too ordinary to excite him.

Then as Olive put her arms around his neck and raised her lips to his, saying in a voice that vibrated with passion:

"Are you going to say goodnight to me?" it seemed ridiculous to ask for anything different.

When he much later left her, he had to admit he had not been disappointed.

She was certainly unusual, and he thought that as her green eyes gleamed at him, she was like a tigress from whom it was impossible for her prey to escape.

Because he wished to assert himself and was determined that no woman, however attractive, should dominate him, it was three days later before once again he accepted an invitation to dine.

This time they were alone.

She attempted now to make her conversation glittering and very amusing, and he thought her provocative *double entendres* were worthy of any French-woman.

Once again she was alluringly dressed and he had to admit that when she was not so modestly gowned, she had the figure of a Greek goddess, and a man would have been inhuman to find fault.

From that moment the Duke found that Olive was with him whatever he did, wherever he went.

But now their idyll was at an end, for tomorrow Lord Brandon would be back.

Once again the Duke found his eye-lids were drooping, and as he threw back the lace-edged silk sheet preparatory to rising, as if dismayed Olive asked:

"You are not leaving, Hugo?"

"It is time I went home," he replied. "Thank you, Olive, for being more exciting than I have ever known you. I shall miss you tomorrow night."

He rose as he spoke and started to dress swiftly and efficiently, having no need, as so many Gentlemen of Fashion had, of the services of a valet.

Olive raised herself a little farther up against the soft pillows embroidered with her initials and surmounted by her husband's coronet and said:

"There is something I want to talk about to you, Hugo."

The Duke was hardly attending.

He had seen by the clock on the mantelpiece that it was nearly two o'clock. He had given orders for his carriage to call for him at exactly that hour, and he disliked being late.

He was, although he had not told Olive, leaving for the country.

He had thought it would be a relief from the scented warmth of her bedroom to feel the clean air on his face, and to know that when he reached his house in Hertfordshire, his horses would be waiting for him.

They would give him the strenuous exercise he needed to get himself back into the peak of condition.

He could see, as he tied his tie, Olive's face in the mirror.

"You know, Hugo dear, that I love you," she was saying, "and I have therefore decided that when George returns tomorrow, I shall tell him about us."

For a moment the Duke thought he could not have heard aright.

Then he turned around and saw that by now Olive was sitting upright, her dark hair falling over her shoulders, and in the heavily curtained bed she looked very alluring.

"What are you talking about?" he asked after a moment.

He spoke lightly, as if he thought she had made a joke and he had somehow missed the point of it.

"I want to marry you, Hugo!" Olive said firmly. "I know that once he is aware that you have been my lover, George will divorce me."

For a moment the Duke was stunned into silence. Then he said, as if it were a remark he had heard before:

"I am afraid, Olive, I am not built to be anyone's husband, and I am quite certain if I did marry you, I should make a most reprehensible one."

"I have worked it all out, Hugo," Olive replied,

and now her voice held a note of steel in it. "I love you, I love you more than I believed it possible to love anybody, and I therefore intend to marry you."

"As you are already married, I am afraid that is impossible," the Duke answered, "and, anyway, I cannot believe you would be so foolish as to throw away the substance for a shadow. As you well know, a divorced woman is irretrievably ostracised by the Society that means so much to you."

"By English Society, I agree," Olive replied. "But you have forgotten the Social World outside this boring island. As the Duchess of Wynchester, I should certainly be accepted in Paris and Rome, and doubtless in every other country in Europe."

"What is more," she went on, "I have not forgotten that your grandmother was Russian, and I am quite certain that if we visited St. Petersburg, we should be welcomed with open arms."

Listening to her speaking firmly in a clear, determined voice which was very different from the passionate tones with which she had been addressing him earlier in the evening, the Duke felt he had stepped into a nightmare.

He could only hope that what she was saying was some amusing trick she was playing on him, but there was a wary look in his eyes and his body was tense as he moved across the room from the mantelpiece to sit down on the side of the bed facing her.

"Now, what is all this about?" he asked. "Are you pulling my leg?"

"On the contrary," Olive declared. "I have thought it out very carefully. I want to marry you, Hugo, I want to be your wife, and once the unpleasantness of the divorce and the first year is over, we will be very, very happy."

"You are crazy!" the Duke exclaimed. "For one thing, you would lose your position here in England, and for another, it is problematical whether the French or any other Europeans, who are very snobby, will accept you."

"They will accept you, dearest," Olive said sweetly, "and therefore ultimately accept me."

There was a little pause before the Duke said, and now his voice had a touch of anger in it:

"Suppose I do not marry you?"

Olive's eyes narrowed and he saw the glint of them.

"You are too much of a gentleman, dearest Hugo," she said, "not to make an honest woman of me. I expect, when he knows the truth, George will call you out, and although it is forbidden, there will be a duel in which inevitably you will be the winner."

She smiled before she added:

"Then after the divorce we can be married in any part of the world you choose, and be together for the rest of our lives."

She spoke as if she were reciting like a child who had learnt a lesson cleverly and was sure of the approval of her teacher.

The Duke rose from the bed to walk to the window and pull aside the curtains as if he felt he must have air.

He could hardly believe that what he had just heard was real and not some wild fragment of his imagination.

10

Then, as he questioned his own sanity, he heard Olive behind him say:

"I love you, Hugo, I love you until nothing else matters except that I should be your wife, and that you should make me yours not just for one or two snatched evenings, but forever!"

The Duke drew in his breath.

So many women had said to him:

"If only we could go on like this for ever!" And invariably on their lips had been the question: "Will you always love me as you do now?"

Why, why, he asked himself angrily, should they always want to tie a man down, keep him captive, and restrict his freedom?

But never, in all his many philanderings, had he been faced with a situation quite so nerve-racking as this one.

He was well aware, as he stared into the night, that he had no wish to marry Olive, and she was, in fact, the last type of woman he desired as a wife.

When he had determined not to marry until he was much older, he had not given much thought to the sort of woman he really would like to bear his name, and, of course, his children.

One thing, however, he did know positively and without any argument was that she would not be in the least like Olive Brandon, or, in fact, the majority of the other women who had pursued him.

He could imagine nothing more unpleasant than to wonder how soon his wife would take a lover, or suspect she was already enticing one of his friends into indiscretions that would offend his pride and the honour of his name.

Now he thought about it, he had always rather despised the women who deceived their husbands by falling into his arms, usually with immodest haste.

Every time he deceived another man by making his wife his mistress he had, although he refused to admit it in so many words, felt as if he, too, were humiliated.

He knew that such an idea would be laughed at by the majority of his friends, and certainly by the raffish set that centred round the Prince of Wales, who was habitually unfaithful to his beautiful Danish-born wife.

He had set the pace and Society had followed him blindly, but, when the Duke thought about it, he knew he had always had reservations in his own mind.

Now he was determined that somehow he must extricate himself from the trap which Olive Brandon had set for him, yawning like a deep chasm in front of his feet, though it was impossible for the moment to think of a way out.

He pulled the curtains to, and turning back, said in a quite calm voice:

"I think, Olive, before you do anything precipitately, we should talk this over. Now is hardly the time, as we are both tired, to make fundamental decisions about our future."

He saw from the expression in her eyes that she was somewhat disconcerted by the way he was speaking, and after a moment she said:

"But, of course, dearest Hugo, if that is what you want, I am agreeable. George will be arriving on the sleeper-train tomorrow morning. I will not say anything to him before the evening. If you will come to tea, when he will be at his Club, we can then make plans."

"I am afraid I cannot come to tea tomorrow," the Duke replied slowly, "as now I am leaving for the country, but I shall be back the following day in time for luncheon."

"You are going to the country at this hour of the night!" Olive exclaimed.

"I have some horses in training, which I particularly want to see," the Duke replied carelessly.

He did not say any more, and after a moment Olive said tentatively:

"Very well, I shall expect you then."

"In the meantime, say nothing to your husband," the Duke insisted.

"To please you, I will agree," Olive conceded. "At the same time, I have no intention of changing my mind. Let me make that quite clear, Hugo, just in case you think we can continue to go on as we are."

It struck him that he had no intention of continuing to go on with her anyway, and at the moment he felt more like strangling her with his bare hands than caressing her.

But the Duke had a firm self-control, which he had acquired over the years by training himself to obey his mind rather than his emotions. As he looked at Olive lying before him in the soft bed, she had no idea of the fury surging through him.

"Very well then," he said, forcing a smile to his lips, "I will call on you on Wednesday, and make sure we are alone."

"But of course, darling," Olive replied. "Would I

want us to be anything else? And you know, my precious, how perfect it will be when we can be together for ever, and there will be no more partings."

She held out both her arms in a gesture of surrender as she spoke, and the Duke took first one of her hands, then the other, and kissed the backs of them.

"Goodbye, Olive," he said. "Sleep well, and once again, thank you for all the happiness we have had together."

"Our happiness is only just beginning," Olive said softly. "A happiness, my wonderful lover, which will be ours for eternity!"

She pulled the Duke towards her as she spoke, but he released her hand, and moving lithely away from the bed, walked towards the door.

"Until Wednesday," he said quietly as he reached it. "And until we have had time to talk together, everything is secret?"

She knew it was a question and she replied:

"I promise it will be so until Wednesday. After that I shall be with you."

She was not certain he heard the last two words because he had passed through the doorway and closed the door quietly behind him.

As he went down the stairs, he wondered how he could ever have been such a fool as to trust Olive when she had said it would be safe to come and make love to her in her house when her husband was away.

Even if he denied the charge, which would be difficult, that she would make against him, it would be substantiated by the servants who had served them at dinner, and the night footman who was now waiting in the hall to let him out.

"How can I have been such an idiot?" the Duke asked as he stepped through the front-door, which the footman held open for him, and went down the steps to where his travelling cabriolet was waiting.

He had arrived in his brougham drawn by two horses, but because he was going to the country, he had ordered the cabriolet to call for him now.

Drawn by four horses, it awaited him, and he knew he would reach his house in Hertfordshire easily within an hour and a half. Then he could go to bed and think over what was awaiting him on Wednesday.

His footman, wearing the Wynchester livery, covered his knees with a rug as he sat back on the comfortable seat. Then the door was closed, the man sprang up on the box beside the coachman, and they set off.

The whole horror of what had occurred swept again over the Duke, and he felt like a wild animal in a trap from which there was no possible way of escape.

How could he have known, how could he have guessed for one second that unlike all the other women with whom he had had passionate *affaires de coeur*, she would dramatise her feelings for him until she demanded marriage.

He knew, if he were honest, it was not only because she thought she loved him—a great many women had given him their hearts—it was also because her position as his wife would be very different from that which she already held.

Even though, as she had obviously worked out, she might never be accepted in English Society, there was no doubt there were a great many places in the world which would welcome the Duke of Wynchester and accept his wife publicly, whatever they might say about her in private.

"I will not marry her, I will not!" the Duke said to himself.

Yet he knew it was almost impossible for him to refuse to do so.

If, as Olive expected, Lord Brandon challenged him to a duel, her name would be bandied about by every gossip from one end of London to the other.

In the circumstances it was an unwritten law that there was nothing a gentleman could do but offer to the woman who had been thus defamed his protection.

As he would also be named publicly in the divorce proceedings, which would have to go through Parliament, he would have no chance of evading the Marriage Service which would follow immediately after it.

The Duke felt as if his head were throbbing and his lips were dry. A thousand unknown pressures were menacing him, but there was nothing he could do about them.

Because he felt restricted and hemmed in, he flung aside the rug with which the footman had covered his knees, and lifting his feet, he put them firmly on the small cushioned seat opposite him.

As he did so, he felt the cushion give a little, and knew the box under it had not been properly fastened.

This annoyed him, because when he travelled for any distance, his valuables were invariably hidden there, and he imagined that the last time the box was emptied it had not been left as secure as it should have been.

But it afforded only a small irritation, and he immediately returned to the problem of Olive.

Too late he knew there had always been something about her that he found unattractive.

Because she had beguiled and bemused him with her passion and her insatiable demand for his love-making, he had not really thought about it clearly, and yet he knew it had been there.

The Duke had been fascinated by many women, and at times had been extremely fond of them.

He had, however, always known that his feelings were not those of the real love which when he was a young man he had sought, telling himself he had no intention of marrying any woman unless he truly loved her.

Perhaps it was the Russian blood in his veins that made him demand more than just the affection and respect which in English circles was accepted as love.

He demanded something which was far more intense, far more spiritual.

His grandmother, a Romanov Princess, had explained to him what love meant in her country.

"A Russian loves with his soul," she said. "It is something of which he is very conscious, and he is not ashamed to speak of it as an Englishman is. He can, of course, love passionately with his body, but when he meets a woman he really loves, then he gives her his soul. That, my dear Hugo, is the love we all seek and which we believe comes from God."

The Duke had been very young when his grandmother had talked to him like that, and yet he had never forgotten it.

After she was dead, he had often wished he had asked her if she thought he would ever find a woman to whom he could give his soul, and who would, of course, love him in return.

But what he was offered was always something very different, and while they laid their hearts at his feet, he knew without asking questions that the heads of the women who said they loved him were screwed on very tightly.

Never in any circumstances would they do anything to damage or sully their position in Society.

That was the test, he told himself, of a love which was basically emotional, that it could be kept secret and undisclosed: while his grandmother had been talking of a love that was very different, a love for which the world would be well lost and never regretted.

He knew, however, that this was not what Olive was offering him.

If he had not been the Duke of Wynchester and very wealthy, she would never for one moment have entertained the idea of accepting the scandal a divorce would cause or throw away her position in England for a man who could not offer her at least as fine, if not a better, position elsewhere.

He told himself now that he might have guessed that she was shrewd, cunning, and calculating.

When he looked back, he could remember little things she had said which might, if he had been more astute, have warned him of the truth.

Instead, he had been lulled into believing that their affair was just like all the others in which he had participated—the enjoyment of two people who desired each other physically, and who, when it was over, could be friends without any recriminations.

He had been wrong, completely wrong, but what could he now do about it?

For a moment all the self-control he had acquired during his thirty-three years of life seemed to crack.

He wanted to scream aloud at his own frustration and, as he had thought already, to strangle Olive before she could tell her husband, as she intended to do, what had been happening between them.

That, the Duke knew, would start the ball rolling and engulf him eventually in a hell of despondency.

How could he bear to give up England and all it meant to him? How could he turn his back on his horses, his houses, and most of all, his friends?

No woman could compensate for such a sacrifice even if he were willing to make it.

Whatever Olive might say about the pleasures they would find in other countries, which he agreed were considerable, he would still yearn for the land to which he belonged, and for the respect and affection of his relatives, and there were a great number of them, who looked up to him as head of the family.

"God, help me out of this mess!" he murmured aloud, and it was a prayer which came from the very depths of his being.

Even as he spoke the words, he felt something strange happening beneath his feet, and for a moment he could not think what it could be.

Then he realised that the soft cushion was rising and the top of the box beneath it was opening.

Considerably startled, the Duke put his feet down on the floor and bent forward to look more closely at what was happening.

While they had been driving away from London, the clouds which had obscured the moon and the stars earlier in the evening had moved away, and now the moonlight shone in through the windows.

To his astonishment, the Duke could see between the cushion on which his feet had rested and the box beneath it a hand appear.

For a moment he thought he must be imagining it, until the lid of the box opened completely and he could see indistinctly, but nevertheless surely, a face.

He sat upright.

"What the devil are you doing here?" he asked.

A small very frightened voice replied:

"I am . . . sorry . . . very sorry . . . but I am being suffocated . . . !"

For an instant the Duke was silent in astonishment. Then he said:

"You did not answer my question—what are you doing here?"

"I heard you . . . say," the voice answered, "when you arrived at Lord Brandon's house, that you were going later to the country . . . and that is where I . . . want to . . . go."

The Duke remembered saying to his footman who had opened the door:

"Make sure the travelling-cabriolet is here at two o'clock. I am going straight to the Castle, so make certain the horses are fresh."

"Yes, Your Grace," the man had replied.

The Duke was aware meanwhile that the face was still peering at him through the open lid of the box in front of him, and he said sharply:

"You had better come out, then I shall be able to put my feet back comfortably where they were before."

"Yes . . . of course."

Something very small seemed to crawl out of the box onto the floor of the carriage, and as the moonlight illuminated it, the Duke was aware, to his astonishment, that it was a girl.

He had not unnaturally thought it must be a boy who was hiding. He remembered when he was young he had often wished to run away from his Tutors and he had assumed that something of the same sort was now happening.

However, crouching down on the rug which he had thrown off his knees was undoubtedly a girl. He could see her eyes were very large, almost unnaturally so, in the small, pointed face, and she had fair hair, so fair that it seemed almost silver in the moonlight.

She was wearing a plain gown in some darkish colour that made her seem very slight and unsubstantial.

She knelt on the floor, looking up at the Duke, and after a moment he said:

"I think you would be more comfortable sitting beside me."

He moved a little as he spoke, and she rose and sat down beside him. As she did so, he realised she was taller than he had first thought her to be.

21

In fact, it was surprising that she had managed to conceal herself in the box opposite.

He picked up the rug from the floor and put it over her knees as he said:

"Now, suppose you tell me what all this is about? I imagine you are running away?"

There was a little pause, then she said:

"What I want is to . . . reach the country . . . but if you wish to stop here and now . . . I can leave you and you . . . need not . . . think about me . . . anymore."

There was a hesitating note in the frightened way in which she spoke, and as the Duke turned to look at her, he found it difficult, while she was sitting beside him, to see her as clearly as when she had been on the floor between the two windows.

"What do you think you would do if I do put you out anywhere on this strange road?" he asked. "Where are you going?"

This time there was quite a long pause before she replied:

"That is . . . my business!"

"I think, as you have taken the liberty of making free of my carriage, it is also mine," the Duke said. "You must be aware that no woman should walk about alone in the middle of the night."

"This is . . . different!"

He hardly heard the words, and yet he knew she said them.

"Why?"

There was no answer, and after a moment he decided he should get her to start from the beginning.

"What is your name?"

"Janeta!"

"You have another name?"

"That is not . . . important."

"I find it quite important," the Duke said. "Suppose you tell me who you are?"

"No one of any interest . . . just a servant in . . . the house from which . . . you have . . . just come."

As she spoke, her words tumbled over one another, and the Duke knew what she had said was untrue.

He turned round to face her and said:

"Your voice is educated, and does not sound to me in the least like that of a servant, so tell me the truth —who are you?"

She looked away from him and he could see her profile against one of the windows.

He had the feeling her features were classical, but he could not be sure.

"I am waiting for an answer, Janeta," he said after a moment, "and I intend to have one."

"Please . . . there is no point in your . . . knowing," she said. "It will only . . . complicate . . . things."

"Why should it do that?"

"Because it will! Please . . . please . . . stop your carriage and let me go . . . away as I want to do . . . just as I had intended to do when you . . . arrive at your . . . Castle."

"And you think no one would see you?"

"No one noticed me . . . climb into your . . . carriage. I am very . . . small."

"I do not think you are as young as I at first imagined you to be," he said, "so I feel responsible for you. Now, as we must start somewhere—I want to know your name."

"Why should it . . . matter to you?"

"For one reason, I am curious," the Duke replied. "Can you not imagine that if our positions were reversed and you found me hidden somewhere, you would wish to know who I was and why I was there?"

"For you it . . . would be . . . different."

"Why?"

"Because you are a man . . . and because . . . life is not . . . difficult where . . . you are . . . concerned."

The Duke thought grimly it was, in fact, very difficult at this particular moment, but there was no point in saying so, and he merely replied:

"If you are having difficulties, I am sure I could solve them. It is something I am rather good at doing where other people are concerned."

That, he thought, was certainly true. He had helped a great number of people in his life in one way or another.

But now he had a problem which for the moment seemed insoluble.

He broke the silence between them by saying:

"Now, let us go back to the beginning—you heard me tell my footman that I was leaving for the country this evening, and you decided to accompany me. That means that you were in front of the house we have just left, and you were therefore living there."

"Not . . . anymore. You have taken me . . . away, and I shall . . . never go . . . back!"

"Why not?"

"I cannot . . . tell you . . . and anyway, you would not . . . understand."

"How do you know until you try me?" the Duke asked. "I have always considered myself a very understanding person. I would like to know why you are running away."

"Because I can stand it no longer . . . because I am being . . . forced to do something which is so unspeakable . . . so horrible . . . so ghastly . . . that I would rather . . ."

The young voice stopped suddenly, and the Duke said quietly:

"You would rather die! Is that what you were going to say?"

The girl did not reply, and after a moment he said:

"Are you telling me that you are going to the country to kill yourself? I do not believe it!"

"You are not to ask . . . questions," she said quickly. "Just stop the . . . carriage and let me . . . get out."

"That is something I have no intention of doing," the Duke answered, "unless you would like me to take you back to London, if that is what you wish."

She gave a cry of horror.

"No, no . . . of course not . . . nothing will make me go back . . . nothing . . . nothing!"

"Very well then, we will go on as long as you tell me why you are leaving."

She turned towards him, and he knew although he could not see her that her eyes were pleading.

"Please . . . do not ask so many . . . questions," she said. "Just let me get out when we . . . arrive and forget I have ever been . . . here and you have ever . . .

seen me. It will be ... embarrassing for you ...
otherwise."

"You mean when I am called to give evidence,"
the Duke persisted.

"This has ... nothing to do with ... you."

"But you have made it my problem and something
that I have to solve," the Duke said. "Janeta, do be
sensible. Now that you had told me so much, tell me
the rest."

"I cannot ... say anymore ... I must not!" she
whispered.

The Duke put out his hand, and unexpectedly took
her chin in his fingers.

She made a convulsive little movement, then was
very still.

He saw she was looking up at him with huge,
frightened eyes, and he could feel her whole body
trembling.

"Now tell me," he said, "who you are, and I intend to have an answer."

Just for a moment he thought she would defy him.
Then in a voice he could hardly hear she said:

"Lady Brandon ... whom you have just been visiting is ... my stepmother!"

"Then you are Lord Brandon's daughter by his
first wife!"

"Yes."

"I had no idea he had any children."

"He had only me," Janeta replied, "and because
Stepmama hates ... me I have been kept away at
School for the ... last four years."

"How old are you?"

"I am eighteen."

"Eighteen?" the Duke repeated. "And with all your life in front of you, you want to destroy it!"

"You . . . do not understand."

"Then make me understand."

"She . . . she says I am to marry a horrible . . . cruel man over whom I think she has some . . . hold. He is very old . . . and lives near Papa's house in the country. He has a . . . reputation which . . . frightens me."

"And you say he wants to marry you?"

"Stepmama found him trying to . . . kiss me. I was struggling and . . . fighting against him . . . and after that she talked to him and he told me I was to . . . m-marry him."

"And you refused?"

"I told him I would not do so . . . then came to London to tell Stepmama that it was something I could not do."

"What did she say?"

"She said I had to, that I had no choice because she would make me . . . and I know that I would rather . . . die!"

The Duke was silent, thinking over what Janeta had said to him. After a moment, as if she felt she must explain herself, she said:

"Last night I went into the Park . . . but there were so many people by the Serpentine and . . . a man spoke to me. I was . . . frightened . . . so I ran home."

"You went to the Park alone!" the Duke exclaimed. "How could you do anything so foolish?"

"I could not think of anywhere else. It seemed a long way to the Thames," Janeta said simply.

27

The Duke did not speak, and after a moment, as if she felt she must go on explaining, she said:

"Tonight I was looking out of a window at the front of the house and wondering whether if I went back to the Park much later, there would be nobody there. Then I heard what you said to your footman, and that was why I hid here in your carriage."

"Now, listen," the Duke said. "I understand your problem, but surely you do not have to marry this man whom your Stepmother has chosen for you? Why do you not talk to your father?"

"For one thing, I do not think Papa would listen to me. He was always disappointed because I was not a boy. I think that was . . . why he married . . . again."

The Duke thought this was very likely the truth, and he said:

"All the same, I cannot believe he would force you into marrying an old man who you say is someone you dislike."

"Papa always does what Stepmama wants of him," Janeta said, "and I would much rather . . . die than marry Major Hodgson."

"Is that his name?"

"Yes. He bought a house near ours, and our grooms told me that he is cruel to his horses and beats them unmercifully."

She paused, then said in a voice that was little above a whisper:

"Also one of the maid-servants told me that he was . . . said to have . . . beaten his wife, which was why she . . . died."

The Duke felt his anger rising.

If there was one thing he loathed more than anything else, it was cruelty, and there was nothing more cruel than sending a child who had heard such stories about a man into his keeping.

"What can I do?" he asked himself. "What the devil can I do about her? Or, for that matter, myself?"

chapter two

THEY drove on for a short while in silence, until the Duke said:

"Why have I never heard about you before?"

He thought, although he was not sure, that Janeta drew in her breath before she replied:

"Stepmama did not want to . . . acknowledge that I even . . . existed. That was why I was sent away to school four years ago and not allowed to come . . . home for the . . . holidays."

"For four years!" the Duke exclaimed.

He could hardly believe such a situation was possible, but Janeta went on.

"I was quite happy with the Nuns, but it was very

lonely being the only girl who appeared to have no family."

The Duke calculated that she must have been fourteen when she went to school, and he asked:

"How old were you when your mother died?"

"I was twelve," Janeta replied, "and for two years it was unutterable misery being . . . without her. Then after Stepmama arrived I was always . . . afraid."

"Afraid?" the Duke questioned in surprise.

There was no answer, and yet he felt her shiver in the same way she had when she spoke of Major Hodgson. Perceptively he asked:

"Are you saying your stepmother was cruel to you? Did she beat you?"

"She . . . hated me because I was . . . Papa's daughter," Janeta murmured in such a low voice he could hardly hear her, "and she beat me . . . herself and engaged a governess for me who was also very . . . unkind."

There was a pain in the young voice which the Duke had never expected to hear in a woman, and he said quickly, as if he could not bear to think about it:

"It must have been a relief to go to school."

"I was ill and our Doctor . . . insisted I leave home," Janeta explained. "I think he . . . understood what was . . . happening."

There was silence as they drove on, and the Duke was thinking of the intolerable position in which Janeta had found herself.

He could understand that having been frightened by being beaten by her Stepmother, now to be told she had to marry a man who was cruel and had a reputation of using a whip on his animals would terrify any woman, let alone someone so young, sensitive, and vulnerable as the girl beside him.

As if she knew what he was thinking, Janeta said suddenly:

"You must not . . . worry over me. Just let me do . . . what I want to . . . do and forget you have . . . ever met . . . me."

"That is impossible," the Duke replied. "Quite impossible! Now we have met and talked, Janeta, you must understand that as I am not entirely without a conscience, I should feel that your death, since that is what you are contemplating, was entirely my fault."

"How could it be?" Janeta asked. "I know now it was very wrong of me to hide in your carriage, but I did not think for a moment that you would find me."

"I expect it was Fate, or perhaps God, who was determined you should not do anything so wicked as to destroy yourself," the Duke said severely.

Janeta gave a little gasp.

"Surely you must understand there is no . . . alternative?" she asked. "Stepmama told me I must go back to the country today and . . . agree to marry Major Hodgson at the . . . end of the month."

Her voice trembled, and then she added:

"She told me that if I did not . . . obey her, she would make me . . . sorry I had ever been . . . born."

There was no doubt from the way she spoke that the threat had terrified her, and the Duke knew that once again she was thinking of being beaten.

It was nothing unusual for parents to beat their children, or to allow their Tutors and governesses to do so, but he could understand that for anyone so

33

frail as Janeta, it would be a torture that would hurt her mentally as well as physically.

He did not know why he was aware of this, although he had been unable to see her properly.

Yet from the way she spoke, and also from her proximity sitting beside him, he was acutely aware of her as a person, and what he was thinking about her was true.

He felt he could, although it seemed strange, look beneath the surface and be aware of her as an individual in a way he could not explain.

It was then he became aware they were driving past a high brick wall, and a moment later the horses turned in through the impressive wrought-iron gates which formed the entrance to the Castle.

It seemed extraordinary that the time had passed so quickly. Yet the Duke knew he had been so intent on thinking about Janeta that he was surprised to find himself home without being bored as he usually was by the long drive from London.

But now they were back, he had to think quickly as to what he should do about Janeta.

As she thought the same thing, she turned towards him and said:

"Let me . . . go."

The words were a little more than a whisper, and the Duke said firmly, his voice almost ringing out in the closed carriage:

"No!"

She turned towards the window, and he knew without her speaking that she was planning, once the carriage came to a standstill, to run away before he could stop her.

He put out his hand and covered hers, feeling her fingers quivering in his grasp like the fluttering of a small, frightened bird.

"I know what you are thinking," he said, "and if you do run away, I shall be obliged, because of what I know you intend to do, to run after you. My servants will follow me, and it will be extremely humiliating."

Janeta drew in her breath, and then she asked like a child who is afraid and unsure of herself:

"Then . . . what can I . . . do?"

"I suggest you stay with me as my guest," the Duke replied. "Tomorrow we will talk over your position and I feel sure I shall find a solution to your problem."

"That is . . . impossible."

"We will talk about it tomorrow," he said firmly. "Nothing, and I mean nothing, is impossible!"

"But how can I . . . stay with . . . you?"

He smiled as he replied:

"Quite easily. Leave all the explanations to me. You will find I am quite imaginative when I have to be."

"You are very kind . . . but I know I should not have . . . involved you in . . . this."

"But I am involved, Janeta," the Duke said, "and now we are here, all you have to do is to obey me and go to sleep for what is left of the night."

As the carriage came to a standstill outside the long row of stone steps which led up to the front door, he added:

"Give me your word of honour that you will still be here in the morning."

Just for a moment Janeta hesitated, until as the Duke's fingers tightened on hers she said with a little sob in her voice:

"I . . . promise."

He knew from the way she spoke she would keep her word, and as the door of the carriage was opened by a footman, the Duke stepped out and turned to help her alight.

He suspected the coachman and footman were looking at her in astonishment.

They walked up the steps, which were covered in red carpet, side by side, to where waiting in the Hall was the Butler and several footmen besides the Duke's secretary, Mr. McMullen.

"Good evening, Your Grace," Mr. McMullen said respectfully, but the Duke did not miss the slight expression of surprise in his eyes as he saw his master was accompanied by a young woman.

"Good evening, McMullen," the Duke said. "I have brought with me an unexpected guest."

As he spoke, he remembered that it would be a mistake to call Janeta by her name.

His servants, and he was sure McMullen also, would be aware of the time he had spent with Lady Brandon, and it was important they should not connect Janeta with her.

He therefore gave Janeta the first name that came into his head as he said:

"Miss Scott has travelled down from London with me and will be staying what is left of the night. Will you arrange that one of the senior housemaids sleeps in the dressing-room next to her bedroom, and tomorrow, unless she leaves us, I will arrange for a more conventional chaperon."

"I understand, Your Grace. Shall I take Miss Scott up to her room?"

"Thank you," the Duke replied. "I am sure she is as eager to go to bed as I am."

"Will you come this way, Miss Scott?" Mr. McMullen asked, moving towards the staircase.

"Goodnight, Janeta," the Duke said lightly. "Sleep well and do not trouble to get up early in the morning."

As she spoke, he looked at Janeta for the first time and saw she was, in a way, very different from what he expected.

In the darkness of the carriage she had seemed so small and young that he had expected her to have the baby-face of a child even though she had told him she was eighteen.

Now he saw that the huge eyes in her heart-shaped face were those of a young woman, and although her body was very slim, almost unnaturally so, the soft curves were those of maturity.

There was, also, he thought, something very different about her from anyone he had ever seen before.

To begin with, her eyes were a very dark blue, and seemed even darker because in her fear the pupils were dilated and almost obscured the colour of them.

Her hair, as he had seen in the carriage, was fair, but not gold as he might have expected with blue eyes, but in the light of the candles almost silver.

It was a strange, almost inhuman little face, and

because she was frightened, Janeta reminded him of the spotted deer in the park who were always hard to tame and rushed frantically away at the first sight of a stranger.

As she looked at him with her large eyes, she seemed to be pleading with him not to leave her.

The Duke smiled at her reassuringly and she turned away to follow Mr. McMullen. But he knew every pulse in her body was tense as she walked up the stairway.

The Duke did not watch her for more than a second, then walked across the Hall into the room in which he habitually sat when he was alone.

As he expected, there was a large amount of papers and correspondence waiting for him on his desk.

He crossed to the other side, where there was a grog table, on which he knew there would be an opened bottle of champagne awaiting his arrival, besides a plate of pâté sandwiches in case he should be hungry after his journey.

He was sure, too, although he did not need it, that his Under-Chef, if not the Senior Chef, was waiting in the kitchen in case he should want something more substantial to eat.

He felt, however, the only thing he needed at that moment was a drink, and he hesitated over whether he should have a strong brandy as being more appropriate for his feelings.

He, however, decided on the champagne, and pouring himself half a glass, drank it down without even tasting it.

Then, knowing Janeta would have been looked after by now, he went up to his own bedroom.

His valet was waiting for him, and having been with the Duke a number of years, he was aware that at this time of night he would not wish to talk.

He therefore assisted him silently, and it was only when he left and the Duke was in the bed that he said:

"Goodnight, Your Grace. It is nice to have you home again."

It was, the Duke thought with a smile, the sort of thing that Hodgson would say. Then, as he lay back against the pillows in the huge four-poster bed in which many generations of his ancestors had been born and died, the problem of Olive Brandon swept over him, and it was like being immersed in the full force of a tidal wave.

He could almost feel her in the darkness menacing him.

He could imagine all too clearly how if she had her way and they came to the Castle as man and wife, she would be sleeping in the Duchess's room and be reigning here and over all his other possessions.

Then he told himself that if he were forced to marry Olive, he would have to leave England never to return, and his whole being cried out against leaving the house he loved, which was redolent of the history of the Chesters all down the ages.

Flags they had captured in battle hung in the Great Hall, and as a boy they were the first thing he looked for when he came home in the holidays.

The pictures of the Dukes who had reigned before

him and the Earl before them hung on the walls in the Great Baronial Hall, up the stairs, and in the Picture Gallery, which filled one wing of the house.

Portraits of their Duchesses hung beside many of them.

They had faces that were beautiful and distinguished, sometimes unattractive, but none of them, the Duke thought to himself, had the craftiness or the self-scheming of Olive Brandon.

"I will not marry her! I will not!" he said aloud in the darkness, and felt as if he could hear her laughing scornfully in that silvery, contrived manner he once thought attractive.

He knew now it should have warned him that everything about her was artificial and insincere.

Strangely, because he had not expected to sleep, he fell asleep while he was hating Olive Brandon with an almost fanatical hatred and awoke to feel exactly the same about her.

Although it had been nearly four o'clock in the morning when he went to bed, Hodgson, as usual, called him at eight o'clock, and as he bathed and dressed, the Duke was not the least tired, but preoccupied with the same problems that had beset him before he went to sleep.

He breakfasted alone, and when he was finishing his coffee, Mr. McMullen came into the room.

"My horses are waiting, McMullen," the Duke said, "so it is no use trying to delay me."

"I had no intention of doing that, Your Grace," Mr. McMullen answered. "I only wondered if, when Miss Scott wakes, and I told the Housekeeper to let her sleep until she did so, you had any message for her."

The Duke glanced at the clock over the mantelpiece and answered:

"I shall be back about eleven-thirty. Tell Miss Scott I will see her in my Study any time before luncheon if she would like to join me there."

"I'll see she gets the message, Your Grace."

The Duke went from the Breakfast Room and found waiting for him, as he expected, outside the front-door, one of the new horses he was training himself.

During the following three hours a series of battles for supremacy between him and an animal which was determined to defy him made him forget everything but the problem of domination in which each was determined to be the winner.

The Duke rode three horses during the morning, each giving him more pleasure than the last.

At the same time, it was impossible not to be conscious of a menacing darkness in the back of his mind which could not be ignored.

As he had told Mr. McMullen, he returned to the house a little after eleven-thirty and went to his Study.

Now he gave his attention to the papers waiting for him on his desk. Yet it was a relief when a quarter of an hour later the door opened and Janeta was shown in.

He had thought that his impressions of her last night were very likely mistaken and were due to their dramatic encounter in the darkness of the carriage, but now he saw her in the daylight, he realised she was indeed very different from anyone he had ever seen before.

She still looked frightened and her blue eyes seemed dark and stormy. He thought he saw her lips tremble a little as she dropped him a curtsy and moved quickly towards the desk where he was sitting.

He rose as she approached him and saw she was wearing the same gown that had seemed dark in the moonlight, but was actually a very soft shade of blue, echoing her eyes.

It was a young girl's dress and very simple. Yet he was aware as he had been last night that it was a woman who confronted him, even though, as he had noticed before, she was extremely thin and her chin bone was sharp against her long neck.

Because he knew she was nervous, the Duke smiled before he said in a deep voice:

"Good morning, Janeta. I hope you slept well."

"When I awoke I could not . . . remember where I was," she answered, "and then I realised I had not thanked . . . you for being . . . so kind to . . . me."

The words seemed to come a little abruptly from her lips and the Duke moved from behind his desk and said:

"Let us sit down and talk. I am sure it will be easier to do so than it was last night."

Janeta followed him to where there was a large velvet sofa in front of a fireplace which because it was summer was filled with a huge arrangement of flowers.

She sat down on the edge of the sofa, clasping her

hands together in her lap and raising her eyes to the Duke.

There was an appealing expression in them which made him aware she was asking silently the same question she had asked last night and for which he had no answer.

He stood with his back to the mantelpiece, looking at her, very smart in his riding-breeches and highly polished riding-boots.

His cravat was tied meticulously, and he wore a whipcord riding-jacket with a yellow waistcoat, the buttons of which were engraved with his crest.

It would be difficult for any woman not to realise what a handsome figure he made, and at the same time an extremely elegant one.

Janeta's eyes, however, were on his face, and after a moment, as if he thought there was no point in not getting to the crux of their difficulties, the Duke said:

"I know that what you are asking me is 'what shall I do?' and that is what we have to decide."

"You would not like me . . . just to go . . . away?" Janeta asked. "It was clever of you to give me a false name so that once I have gone no-one here will . . . connect me with Papa or my . . . Stepmother."

The way she spoke the last word told the Duke all too clearly how terrified she was of Olive Brandon, and he thought it ironical that he was almost in the same state that she was.

"Surely," he said after a moment, "you have some relation, perhaps on your mother's side of the family, with whom you could live."

"I did think of that," Janeta said, "but before I

went to school, Stepmama prevented me from writing or seeing any of my relations. She does not want them to think about me, especially now that I am home."

She looked away from the Duke as she spoke and said:

"Perhaps you will think it strange that I came home knowing I should be . . . unwelcome. But the Nuns would not . . . keep me any . . . longer."

"Why not?" the Duke asked.

"I was the oldest girl in the school, and when I won almost all the prizes last term, I knew they thought it unfair on the other pupils."

The Duke smiled.

"So you are clever, Janeta?"

"If I were," Janeta answered in a different voice, which had a passionate note in it, "I would not have . . . burdened you with my troubles . . . but would have died as I . . . intended to do, in the . . . Serpentine."

He knew as she spoke that she was not being dramatic, just simply blaming herself for having run away, because it was dark, because there were people there, and a man had spoken to her.

He found it incredible to think of any young girl in the same social position as Janeta having to suffer such unpleasant experiences, and being treated as she had been by her stepmother.

But, he was aware that young girls were very often married off almost as soon as they left the school-room and had little say as to whose wife they should be.

For any social mother, it was a feather in her cap

for her daughter to make a good marriage, and whether the daughter thought the man chosen for her was attractive or not was immaterial.

Thinking it over, the Duke could understand that in Olive's desire to be rid of an unwanted stepdaughter, she would tolerate no competition in her own home, and would be prepared to marry Janeta to the first man who approached her.

The fact that he did not move in the same social world as she did was, of course, an advantage.

As the Duke was silent while he was thinking this out, Janeta, watching him, said after a moment:

"How can you . . . allow me to . . . trouble you in this . . . way? I know what a . . . nuisance I am being, so . . . may I please . . . make a . . . suggestion?"

The Duke sat down in an armchair opposite her, and crossing his legs, said:

"Of course. We said we would talk this out, and that is what we must do. What is your suggestion?"

"I have been thinking," Janeta said, "that if you will not allow me to . . . kill myself . . . though that would make things . . . easier for everyone, then perhaps I could go . . . somewhere where I am quite unknown and find . . . some work to do."

"Work?" the Duke questioned. "What sort of work?"

She made a little helpless gesture with her hands before she said:

"I have been well educated, I am sure I could teach children, or since the Nuns insisted that we should sew beautifully, I think I could make quite a number of things which people would buy from me."

She spoke courageously, yet the Duke was still aware of the fear behind every word she said.

Also, he had not missed the fact that her fingers were lacing and unlacing each other as she spoke, and were trembling as they had last night when he had laid his hand on hers.

He settled himself a little more comfortably in the chair before he said:

"Now, listen, Janeta, you know as well as I do that you are too young and far too inexperienced to live alone. If you were to put any of these ideas into operation, then you would have to live with someone who would look after you and protect you, if from nothing else, from starving to death."

Janeta looked down and he saw her eyelashes were dark against the white of her skin.

Then she said:

"It must seem to you very . . . presumptuous, but as I have . . . nothing with me, only what I stand up in and . . . no money, I am afraid I shall have to ask you to . . . lend me a little, but of course . . . once I was earning I would . . . pay it back."

He thought that was how he had expected she would feel, and remembered how many women had asked him without scruple to give them jewellery and furs, and even in one or two instances to buy them houses.

But none of them had ever suggested for one moment that the money he had spent on their behalf should be repaid.

"I am not worrying," he said aloud, "about what the cost might be, Janeta—that is immaterial—but what would be the best thing for you to do."

She did not answer, and once again he knew she was thinking that from the windows of her bedroom she had seen his lake, which lay in front of the Castle.

It was a very large and very beautiful one, and was fed by a broad stream which ran into it at one end, flowing out as a cascade at the other, and ending in a whirlpool which was known to be dangerous.

Because what he was thinking upset him, he rose from the chair and said:

"The way we are talking is ridiculous. There are only two things we can do if we are to be sensible. The first would be for me to take you back to your father and explain to him—and I would be very eloquent on the subject—that this sort of situation must not occur again and that you have no intention of marrying a man that your Stepmother has chosen for you."

He spoke sharply, but almost before he could finish the last sentence, Janeta sprang to her feet with a shrill cry.

"How can you say such a thing?" she asked. "How can you take me back? For if you do, whatever Papa promises, Stepmama will have . . . her way as she . . . always does!"

She stood facing him defiantly as she spoke, and then her hands went up to her eyes and the Duke knew she was crying.

"I am sorry, Janeta," he said. "I should not have put the idea to you so bluntly."

"I . . . cannot go back. You . . . do not . . . understand. She will never . . . forgive me because I have told . . . you what has . . . happened."

The Duke thought this was true, and it was something he had overlooked.

Janeta's eyes were still covered with her hands, and he said:

"Forget what I said. It was very foolish of me. Please stop crying, I cannot bear tears."

Janeta groped for a handkerchief she could not find, and the Duke took one from the breast pocket of his riding-jacket and held it out to her.

She wiped her eyes unselfconsciously as a child might have done, then blew her tiny nose and sat down again in the chair she had just vacated, with the handkerchief in her lap.

Then, as she looked up at him, her eyelashes wet and the tear stains still on her cheeks, the Duke thought no-one could look more pathetic and more in need of care and protection.

"The other suggestion," he said after a moment, "I had in mind was that I should find you someone with whom you could live, and who, if that is what you wished, would never have any idea of your true identity. Yet how can you really face a lifetime of living under a shadow of being Miss Nobody from Nowhere?"

He paused before he went on:

"I can foresee endless complications, endless questions which cannot be answered, and the situation would be intolerable for an older woman, let alone someone of your age."

"Anything . . . would be . . . better than having . . . to go back," Janeta said hesitatingly. "But I am frightened that . . . Stepmama might try to . . . find me, just to make sure . . . I was not doing anything of which she might . . . not approve. Once she has made up her mind . . . she always gets . . . her own way."

It struck the Duke that that was exactly what he was afraid of as concerned himself. Without really being aware what he was doing, he walked to the window and looked out over the flower-beds and shrubs brilliant with colour against the green lawns which sloped down to the lake.

Across the water, glimmering gold in the sunshine, he could see the great oak trees which had stood there for hundreds of years with the spotted deer lying in the shade beneath them.

This, he thought, was what Olive intended to take away from him. This was what she would force him to give up unless he could extricate himself from the trap in which she had caught him.

He felt as if his whole being were crying out 'Save me! Save me!' and it was a cry for help that must somehow find an answer, and quickly.

Thinking of himself, he had almost forgotten Janeta was behind him until a quiet, trembling little voice said:

"I am . . . sorry, so . . . very, very . . . sorry to . . . worry you like . . . this."

The Duke turned around. He saw the small frightened face with thin, pale cheeks and the long fingers which trembled as they held his handkerchief.

He stood looking at her, and then almost as if a blinding light encircled her, he knew she was his salvation.

She was the answer to his cry for help.

Slowly he walked back to where he had stood before in front of the mantelpiece. His face was very grave, but for the first time that day there was an expression of hope in his eyes that had not been there before.

"Now, listen, Janeta," he said. "I have an idea."

chapter three

As Janeta raised her eyes to his, the Duke felt for words. Then slowly he said:

"As it happens, I am rather in the same position as you are. You are being forced into marriage with someone you dislike, and I am being pressured into marrying a woman who I know would not make me a good wife."

Janeta stared at him, and then she said:

"But surely . . . it is easy for . . . you to say . . . no."

The Duke smiled.

"Is it not as easy as it sounds. In fact, and I have no intention of going into detail, it will be very, very difficult for me to extricate myself from a very unfortunate situation unless you help me."

Janeta was so surprised that her eyes seemed to grow larger than ever in her pale face before she said:

"Is it . . . possible that I could . . . help you?"

"You could be very helpful if you agree to what I suggest," the Duke replied, "and I know it will help you too."

"You know I would do . . . anything," Janeta murmured.

Now her voice died away as if she felt it would be foolish for her to say anything, but she should just listen to the Duke.

He drew in his breath before he said:

"What I am going to suggest, Janeta, is that we announce that we intend to be married. In other words, we become engaged."

He knew by the expression on Janeta's face that she could not believe she had heard him aright, and he went on quickly:

"It will, of course, only be a pretended engagement, one which will last only as long as we both wish it to, in fact until we are both out of danger. Then we can say that we find, after all, that we are not as compatible as we had thought, and we will both be free."

There was a silence before Janeta said:

"I understand what you are saying, or I think I do, but I know that Stepmama will be furiously . . . angry at the idea that you might . . . wish to . . . marry me."

The Duke knew from the way she spoke that she had a shrewd idea of what his relations were with her Stepmother.

It would be impossible, since she was living in the house, for her not to realise that when her father was away, he and Olive were together almost every day and on a number of occasions dined alone.

He did not wish to think of it further, but he had the uncomfortable idea at the back of his mind that since servants always talk, Janeta would have found it hard not to listen.

To carry off an awkward moment, he said loftily:

"Whatever your Stepmother may think, I am sure your father will welcome me as a son-in-law. We often meet on race-courses and we both belong to the same Club."

He did not add, although he knew it was true, that any parent in the whole of England would welcome him, with his title, his money, and possessions as a son-in-law, and thought it extremely unlikely that Lord Brandon would be an exception.

"I am . . . sure that . . . what you are saying is . . . true," Janeta said in a hesitating little voice, "but Stepmama will be very . . . very angry."

"She may be angry," the Duke said, "but I think we can try to be clever so that you have nothing, or very little, to do with her. I am going to take you out driving this afternoon, which I think you will enjoy, and then to call on my Grandmother at the Dower House."

Janeta looked at him with troubled eyes and he went on:

"She is very old, and although she seldom goes out, she enjoys meeting new people and I know she will be pleased not only to meet you, but to invite you to stay with her."

Janeta started, and she said involuntarily:

"Oh . . . please . . . must I leave . . . you?"

"Only until our engagement is announced and I can find one of my younger relatives to chaperon you here in the Castle."

Janeta looked away from him.

"I can see once again . . . I am being a . . . terrible nuisance . . . to you," she said unhappily.

"On the contrary, you are my life-line in a rough sea when I very badly need one."

"Is that really . . . true?"

"I promise you it is, and now we have settled our immediate future, let us enjoy ourselves and for the moment forget our troubles."

He hoped Janeta would smile at him eagerly as any other woman would have done, but instead she said:

"I think your plan is a very clever one . . . at the same time, I am . . . afraid it will not . . . succeed."

"For you or for me?" the Duke asked.

She did not answer, and he said in a different tone of voice:

"Now, come along, no more gloom. We have a little time before luncheon and you must tell me which you would rather see, my pictures or my horses."

Now there was definitely a light in Janeta's eyes that had not been there before.

"I want to see both," she said, "but if you think that is very greedy of me, perhaps I should see the pictures first in case I am unable to enter the Castle again."

"I promise you will enter it many times, and I

have said that once I have the right chaperon for you, you can stay here."

He knew she was very excited by the idea, and he held out his hand as if to a small child and said:

"Come along, we will go to the Picture Gallery first and you can tell me what you think of my collection, which I am assured by everyone is one of the finest in England."

"Of course it is," Janeta replied.

"Why, of course?"

"Because everything about you is so perfect, so exactly as it should be, that I keep thinking you are not real."

The Duke laughed, and it was a spontaneous sound.

"That is the nicest compliment I have ever had," he said, "and I hope, Janeta, you will continue to think the same when you know me better."

He took her into the Picture Gallery that ran the whole length of one wing, and as he expected she was entranced by the pictures.

What did surprise him was that she knew so much about them. In fact, in some cases when they discussed the artist she knew more about his life and work than he did.

She also had original ideas about each masterpiece, which were very different from the gushing and trite remarks of the women to whom he had shown his collection in the past.

He had known then that when they apprised a picture and spoke of it in glowing terms, they were really speaking of himself. Every word each one uttered and every look given him was a deliberate enticement for him to appreciate the woman speaking.

As they walked the whole length of the Gallery, he was aware, and it rather amused him, that Janeta had eyes only for the pictures, and for her he was just a well-informed guide who could tell her what she wished to know.

Long before they had finished the Gallery, let alone looked at the other rooms where the Duke had also hung his pictures, luncheon was announced.

They sat together in the large Baronial Dining Hall with its Minstrel Gallery at one end and at the other the huge stone medieval fireplace which had been carved for one of the earlier Earls of Chester.

Because Janeta wanted to know the history of everything she saw, the Duke searched his memory for stories which he had heard as a boy and had half-forgotten in the passing years.

To his surprise, the luncheon, which was quite a large one, seemed to pass far quicker then he had expected, and he found he had enjoyed having such an appreciative audience who listened attentively to everything he said.

After luncheon he had his Phaeton brought round, drawn by a pair of magnificent chestnuts which matched each other exactly, and which he had bought recently at a private sale.

He not only enjoyed driving them, but Janeta's appreciation of them. They drove through the woods and along the stream which fed the lake.

The Duke explained the alterations and improvements he was making to the Estate and found to his surprise that Janeta was genuinely interested.

He was used to women listening to him because he was an attractive man. But he was well aware that the subjects he spoke of were immaterial so long as ultimately the conversation got back to their feelings for him, which of course were expressed in just one word, which was—love.

Now he discovered, unless she was a consummate actress, that Janeta was really eager to learn about the rotation of crops and was thrilled with the brood mares they inspected in one of the fields, several of which had their newly born foals with them.

Only when the Duke turned his horses towards a house she had not seen before did he feel her body tense and knew once again she was afraid.

"My grandmother is over eighty years old," he said "and most people find her rather formidable, but I want you to try not to be afraid of her but just be happy until I return from London tomorrow."

"You are . . . going to . . . London?" Janeta asked.

"To see your father," the Duke replied, "and of course to ask him if I may pay my addresses to you. I cannot believe he will refuse me."

There was a faintly sarcastic note in what he had said, because he knew only too well from what Olive had told him that Lord Brandon was not as wealthy as she could wish.

He was, therefore, quite certain that the advantage of having an exceedingly wealthy son-in-law would not go unnoticed.

There was a little pause after he had spoken, and then Janeta said in a very low voice:

"Suppose Papa will not . . . allow us to be . . . engaged."

The way she spoke told the Duke she was really thinking of her Stepmother, and he, too, was thinking of Olive.

However, he was sure his plan was the perfect answer to her intention of forcing her husband to divorce her. He would get his story in first and that would explain why he had visited the house so often.

It would be impossible after he had declared his wish to marry Janeta for Olive to make her tale credible.

"I have been clever, very clever," the Duke told himself, and he was smiling as he drove his horses up the short drive to the Dower House.

It was an attractive building, built in the reign of Queen Anne, and as the groom ran to the horses' heads and the Duke helped Janeta down, he knew because her fingers were cold and trembling that she was still frightened.

An aged butler with dead white hair escorted them across the Hall and into a Drawing-Room which looked out over a rose-garden with a sun-dial in the centre of it.

Sitting in the window in the sunshine was an elderly woman who gave a little cry of delight when the Duke was announced.

"Hugo, my dear boy," she exclaimed, "this is a surprise and I am delighted to see you!"

"I am glad about that, Grandmama," the Duke said, kissing her cheek. "I have come in fact to ask your help in looking after Janeta Scott, as I have to leave for London tomorrow morning."

"Janeta Scott?" the Dowager Duchess exclaimed.

"I do not think I have heard you speak of her before."

There was an enquiring look in the old lady's eyes as she saw how young Janeta was.

"Tell me about yourself, my dear," she said as Janeta rose from a curtsy. "It is unusual for my grandson to have anyone so young staying with him at the Castle."

"I thought that might surprise you, Grandmama," the Duke interposed, "and now I will let you into a secret. Janeta and I wish to become engaged, but first I have to approach her father, Lord Brandon, and ask his permission."

"Lord Brandon?" the Dowager Duchess repeated.

There was a quizzical look in her eyes which told the Duke without words that the name Brandon certainly meant something to her, and he suspected she had heard rumours of his *affaire de coeur* with Olive.

Although she lived quietly in the country, the Dowager had innumerable friends in the social world who kept her informed of all the latest gossip, especially when it concerned him.

"Janeta's real name, as I expect you know, Grandmama," the Duke went on, "is Brand, but for reasons which I shall explain to you another time, she stayed last night at the Castle as Janeta Scott, and until I return from London tomorrow with her father's approval, I want her to be known here in your house as Miss Scott."

"If there is one thing I love," the Dowager Duchess said, "it is a mystery, but I also prefer it to be solved for me."

"You will have to wait," the Duke said. "Then

Grandmama, you shall be the first to know exactly what is happening."

He thought as he spoke that he should have warned Janeta before they had arrived that she would have a lot of questions to answer.

Then to make it easier for her he elaborated on what he had just said.

"The truth is, Grandmama, that Janeta has been very unhappy with her Stepmother, and so I spirited her away from London without anybody being aware of what I was doing."

He paused, but as the Duchess did not speak, he went on:

"We did not have time for her to pack anything, so I have brought her to stay with you without any clothes and can only ask you to be kind enough to manage as best you can until, as I hope, I may bring several trunks back with me when I return from visiting her father."

"It certainly sounds the beginning of a dramatic tale," the Dowager Duchess said, "and naturally you can trust me to keep your secret, at least for the moment. Actually there is no-one here at present to whom I could talk except your cousin Emily, who is as deaf as a post and anyway never listens to anything I say."

The Duke laughed. He was used to his grandmother finding fault with her relations and declaring that all of them, with the exception of himself, were exceedingly dull.

But Janeta still looked worried.

"I hope, Ma'am," she said in a low voice, "you

will not find it a . . . nuisance having me to stay . . . unexpectedly."

"Of course not," the Dowager Duchess replied. "I am delighted, dear child, not only to have you with me, but to be a part of this intriguing tale."

Her eyes twinkled as she looked at her grandson and said:

"You had better be careful, Hugo, or you will be taken before the magistrates for abducting a minor."

"If I am," the Duke replied lightly, "I shall look to you, Grandmama, to bail me out and save me from being imprisoned."

He had tea with his Grandmother and Janeta, and when he rose to leave, he saw a desperate look in Janeta's blue eyes that made him say:

"Will you allow me, Grandmama, to have a few words in private with Janeta before I go?"

"That is something I quite expected you to ask," the Dowager chuckled. "Of course you want to be alone with her. Take her into the Morning-Room. No-one will disturb you there."

"Thank you," the Duke said.

He kissed his Grandmother's cheek, and then with Janeta beside him crossed the Hall to the Morning-Room, which was a small, attractive room looking out over another part of the garden.

As they entered it and he shut the door, Janeta said:

"When will you be back?"

"As soon as I possibly can," the Duke replied. "I intend to see your father as soon as he comes downstairs for breakfast."

"That will be at eight-thirty," Janeta said. "He is never late and he will be alone."

The Duke was already aware of that, knowing that Olive never rose before, as the servants put it, "the world was well-aired."

Aloud he replied:

"That is what I thought. I shall be able to talk to him without any interference."

He saw Janeta's eyes were still troubled and he went on:

"The moment your father gives his consent, I will arrange to have it put in the *London Gazette* and *The Morning Post*. Then once we are officially engaged, nothing need disturb you, and you can forget your troubles and I can forget mine."

He spoke lightly and he thought Janeta would smile at him. However, she still looked troubled and after a moment he asked:

"What is worrying you?"

"I cannot help feeling," Janeta said, "that it will not be as . . . easy as you think it . . . will be."

The Duke told himself he was not thinking it would be easy, because he knew that Olive would not only be furiously angry, but also murderously frustrated.

But there would be nothing she could do, and even if in her fury she blurted out that he and she had been lovers, he did not think for a moment that Lord Brandon would believe her, nor that actually would she dare to gamble on the hope that she might convince him.

What was more, once the engagement to Janeta was announced, whatever she said, and however spiteful she might be, everyone would be certain it was just jealousy and would not take her seriously.

"Leave everything to me, Janeta," he said. "All you have to do is forget how unhappy you have been, and I promise the future will be very different."

He thought she was thinking about what would happen when their engagement was terminated, and after a moment he said:

"There is no hurry for us to do anything except make everyone believe that we are in love and looking forward to being married. In six months' time, perhaps sooner if you wish, it will be easy to plan what we can say and how we can find somewhere for you to live without coming into contact with your stepmother."

"You are ... very kind," Janeta said in a low voice. "I know you are thinking of me ... and no-one since Mama died has been so ... kind and ... considerate."

There were tears in her eyes as she went on:

"I shall pray very ... very hard while you are ... away that I shall be able to ... help you as you are helping ... me."

"That is exactly what I want you to do," the Duke said, "and I am sure your prayers will be heard. Do not worry, Janeta, everything will be all right. Now, come and see me off."

He put out his hand to take hers as he had done before, and as she took it, Janeta raised it to her lips.

Then as the Duke wondered if he should kiss her in return, she wiped her eyes and said in a different voice:

"Please, if it is possible, bring me some of my

clothes back with you. I shall feel very . . . embarrassed borrowing . . . everything from your Grandmother."

The Duke opened the door of the Morning-Room.

"I shall do my best," he said, "and I shall hope to be back here tomorrow in time for luncheon, or certainly for tea."

The servants were waiting in the Hall, and he walked out through the front-door and climbed into his phaeton.

As he picked up the reins, he looked back at Janeta and saw her standing a little forlornly at the top of the steps, and he had the idea there were tears once again in her eyes.

As he drove away, she waved to him and he raised his hat, finding himself thinking that she took things far too seriously for a girl of her age.

During their pretended engagement he would do his best to see she had the parties and amusements to which she was entitled as a débutante, but from which Olive had lamentably decided to exclude her.

The thought of Olive made the Duke frown, and now he was thinking that, although his plans seemed foolproof, he could not believe she would accept such a situation without trying to make trouble.

Once again he found his anger rising inside him as he remembered the determination in her voice when she had said she intended to marry him and described how she had thought it all out so precisely, and, at the same time, although he hated to admit it, cleverly.

"This will teach me a lesson," he told himself as he drew nearer to the Castle, "never to trust a woman, and never again to make myself vulnerable to what is sheer blackmail of the very foulest sort."

Back at the Castle he had dinner alone and went to bed early. He did not sleep, going over and over very carefully in his mind what he should say to Lord Brandon.

He was called as dawn broke and by six-thirty he was already on his way to London.

His horses covered the miles quickly and he had time to go to his own house when he arrived to wash as well as change his horses before he drove round to Brandon House in Park Lane.

The footman who opened the door seemed surprised to see him, but he walked into the Hall saying:

"Is His Lordship in the Breakfast-Room?"

"Yes, Your Grace."

"Then please announce me."

The footman was too flustered to do anything but what he was told, and he opened the door of the Breakfast-Room saying:

"His Grace the Duke of Wynchester, M'Lord."

Lord Brandon, who was sitting at the table reading *The Times,* looked up in surprise.

The Duke walked forward to say:

"Good morning, My Lord. Forgive me intruding on you so early, but I have driven up from the country specially to see you and I wondered if I might join you."

"Of course, my dear fellow," Lord Brandon replied. "Help yourself and tell me why you have come."

The Duke went to the sideboard on which there was a row of silver entrée dishes, and as he helped himself, a servant hastily laid a place for him at the table.

The Duke sat down, and when a cup of coffee had been set by his side, he asked:

"How was the fishing?"

"Very good indeed," Lord Brandon said with satisfaction. "We got over forty in the fortnight, nineteen to my own rod!"

"That was very good," the Duke said, "and what are the shooting prospects this year?"

Lord Brandon went into a long exposition on the breeding of grouse, the condition of the heather, and the hopes of exceptional bags in the autumn.

By the time he had finished speaking, the servants had left the room, and they were alone.

"I wonder," the Duke said, "why you do not have a moor of your own in the North, seeing how fond you are of shooting."

"It is something I would very much like," Lord Brandon replied, "but unfortunately I cannot afford both a moor and to keep up this house in London."

"Well, I hope you will come and shoot with me in August," the Duke said. "My river is not as good as the Tay, but my moors are certainly the equal if not better than Kilkennys."

"It is an invitation I am delighted to accept." Lord Brandon smiled.

"And I hope you will be even more pleased to do so," the Duke said, "when I tell you the reason I am here this morning is to ask you to give your blessing on my engagement with your daughter, Janeta."

For a moment Lord Brandon stared at him almost open-mouthed. Then he exclaimed:

"Janeta! But I had no idea you knew the girl. She

66

has only just returned from abroad, where she was at school."

"I have seen quite a lot of her while you have been away," the Duke said, "and as we find we have many things in common and everyone tells me it is time I settled down, I am here to ask you formally for Janeta's hand in marriage."

Lord Brandon forced the astonishment from his eyes and there was a smile on his lips which seemed to illuminate his face as he said:

"I have never dreamt of such a thing, but of course, young man, I am delighted, absolutely delighted for you to marry Janeta."

The Duke inwardly gave a sigh of relief and began to eat his breakfast with relish.

"I have, of course," Lord Brandon was saying, "hoped that Janeta would make a good marriage, but I never dreamt, it never entered my mind, that she would marry you. As I have said, I have not seen much of her during the last years, but my first wife was a very lovely woman, and Janeta resembles her."

The Duke was finishing his coffee when the door of the Dining-Room opened, and to his astonishment Olive came in.

If he was surprised, so was Lord Brandon.

"My dear!" he exclaimed. "You are up very early."

"I heard you had a visitor," Olive replied, "which was definitely a surprise."

The questioning way in which she spoke told the Duke she was suspicious that something was going on behind her back and she was determined to find out what it was.

His experience of women also told him that she had dressed in a great hurry, for her hair, instead of being arranged in the usual elaborate fashion, was caught back into a bun at the back of her head.

Nevertheless, with her green eyes glinting against her magnolia skin, she looked exceedingly beautiful, but also as dangerous as a cobra.

Now, as if she were determined to get to the point, she said to the Duke:

"What brings Your Grace here so early in the morning?"

"Wynchester has come with good news, Olive," Lord Brandon interrupted before the Duke could reply. "I know you will be as surprised as I am, but he tells me he and Janeta wish to be married and he has asked my permission, which, of course, I have given him, to announce their engagement."

The Duke watched with some anxiety Olive's re-action to this announcement.

He saw her body grow tense, and as she drew in her breath, he thought for one terrifying moment that she was going to scream out the truth that he was her lover.

Then her eyes narrowed, and almost as if he could see her brain working, he knew she was thinking swiftly of how she could prevent him from marrying her stepdaughter and was utterly and completely de-termined to do so.

"I knew you would be pleased, my dear," Lord Brandon was saying. "In fact, before I went away you were insistent that Janeta, having returned from abroad, should be married. I thought myself it was too soon, but, of course, Wynchester has changed my mind."

Olive drew in her breath and then she said slowly but distinctly so that the words seemed to ring out around the room:

"What a pity! What a terrible pity it is that His Grace is too late!"

"What do you mean, too late?" Lord Brandon asked sharply.

"I was going to tell you, darling," Olive said, "but there has been no time since your return, that dear little Janeta and Harold Hodgson told me just after you had left for Scotland that they wished to be married, and were, of course, very much in love."

"Hodgson? Who do you mean by Hodgson?" Lord Brandon asked. "Not that chap who lives near us at home?"

"Yes, of course. You know Major Hodgson, such a nice man, and completely infatuated with your daughter."

"But he is old, much too old," Lord Brandon said, "and besides . . ."

"He is younger than you, darling," Olive said sweetly, "and no-one could call you an old man. And I thought someone a little older than herself would look after Janeta, and prevent her from making the mistakes that so many young girls make without a man to guide and protect them."

"Well, I have told Wynchester he can marry her, and that is that," Lord Brandon said.

The Duke, who had been holding his breath, felt himself relax.

Then Olive, in a coaxing voice he knew so well, said, leaning towards her husband:

"Oh, but darling, I am afraid in your absence I gave my permission to Major Hodgson and, of course, to dear Janeta, that they should be engaged."

"It was for me to do that," Lord Brandon said gruffly.

"I never dreamt, I never thought for a moment that you would not wish your daughter to be happy," Olive said, "and they were so insistent that they were in love and you have always trusted me in affairs of the heart."

"That is all very well . . ." Lord Brandon began, but Olive continued:

"It is you, George dear, who taught me that an Englishman's word is his bond, and I cannot believe that you would want Janeta, having given her word that she will marry Harold Hodgson, to go back on it just because she has a better offer. It would seem very dishonourable and not worthy of your name."

"Well, if you put it like that," Lord Brandon began.

It was then the Duke intervened to say:

"I think, My Lord, that Lady Brandon has misunderstood Janeta's feelings. She told me that although it had been suggested to her that she should marry this man Hodgson, she was horrified at the idea and in fact contemplated running away rather than have anything to do with him."

"Is this true?" Lord Brandon asked, only to be interrupted by a shrill laugh from Olive.

"Is that what the naughty little girl told you?" she asked the Duke. "Oh, well, we must forgive her lying, for what woman, young or old, could resist the glamour and allure of becoming a Duchess?"

"I think the best thing," Lord Brandon said heavily, "is for me to talk to Janeta. By the way, where is she? I have not seen her since I came back."

"I took her away with me," the Duke said, "and she is at the moment staying with my Grandmother in the Dower House at Wynchester."

He saw the fury in Olive's eyes as he spoke, and then she said:

"I think you have taken a great deal upon yourself, Duke! In fact I am surprised that you did not ask my permission."

"As a matter of fact, that is exactly what I came here today to do," the Duke replied blandly.

"Well, I want to see Janeta and talk to her," Lord Brandon said. "The sooner she comes home the better."

"You are quite right, darling," Olive agreed in a cooing voice, "but I know how punctilious you are where affairs of honour are concerned, so I think if we send for Janeta, we should also ask Major Hodgson to visit us."

As she spoke, she reached across the table and put her hand on her husband's. He looked into her green eyes and was lost.

"Of course, if that is what you think is right," he said.

"I do," Olive said, "and I knew you would agree with me."

She turned towards the Duke and said:

"Would you be kind enough to have my stepdaughter conveyed here as soon as possible—perhaps this afternoon."

"As it happens," the Duke said slowly, "I have an engagement this afternoon which is impossible for me to cancel."

He looked at Olive as he spoke and he knew she thought he was referring to his promise to call on her at tea-time."

"I will, however," he went on, "bring Janeta back tomorrow morning. Shall we say by noon?"

"Yes, yes," Lord Brandon agreed. "Noon will be soon enough, and I regret, Wynchester, that things are not so plain-sailing as they seemed when you first arrived."

The Duke rose to his feet.

"I can only hope," he said, walking around the table to hold out his hand to Lord Brandon, "that you and your wife will sort things out and decide to make me a very happy man."

"I hope so too," Lord Brandon answered.

At the same time, he gave a side-long glance at Olive which told the Duke without words that once they were alone, she would get her way.

He bowed to her, saying:

"Good-bye, Lady Brandon, I shall look forward to our meeting."

He knew as he spoke she was assuming he was again referring to their meeting that afternoon, and there was a little smile of triumph on her lips as she watched him walk towards the door and let himself out.

The Duke got into his carriage which was waiting

outside and gave the coachman directions to where he wanted to go.

Then, as the horses drove off, he told himself that after he had seen Olive's behaviour that morning, he would fight to the death rather than have her for his wife.

chapter four

THE Duke did not arrive back at the Dower House until after nine o'clock.

As his Grandmother dined very early, and usually in her room, he was afraid that Janeta might have gone to bed.

As he stepped down from his phaeton, his highly polished Hessians slightly dusty, he said to the old butler:

"Is Miss Scott still up?"

"She's in the Drawing-Room, Your Grace, and we've all been worried in case Your Grace'd had an accident."

The Duke smiled.

"No, Jackson," he answered, "it was nothing like that, and I have arrived home safe and sound."

"That's good news, Your Grace," Jackson said, who had known him since a boy.

He was leading the way across the Hall as he spoke, moving very slowly because he suffered from rheumatism.

The Duke followed him until they reached the door of the Drawing-Room, then he walked in without waiting to be announced.

Janeta was seated on the sofa with a book in her hands, but as he entered, the Duke was aware perceptively that she was not reading it, but staring sightlessly across the room with the frightened expression in her eyes which he knew so well.

She turned her head as he entered, and when she saw who it was, jumped up and ran towards him.

"You are back!" she cried. "I have . . . been so . . . worried . . . so desperately . . . worried in case . . . something had . . . happened."

The pause between the words told the Duke what she was thinking, and he said quietly:

"I am sorry you have been worried."

"And your Grandmother . . . was worried too," Janeta said. "She was sure because you were so late you must have had an . . . accident, but I thought that was unlikely, seeing how well you drive."

It was not really a compliment, and the Duke knew she was wondering feverishly how Olive had delayed him so much longer than he had intended, and if, in fact, he was bringing her bad news.

Her eyes searched his face, and he said again in a quiet voice:

"Come and sit down, Janeta, I want to talk to you."

She obeyed him, and he had the feeling that although she was outwardly composed, she was trembling inside.

The Duke was just about to speak, when Jackson came into the room followed by a footman carrying a tray on which there was a bottle of champagne and a plate of sandwiches.

"I thinks Your Grace'd need something after that long drive," Jackson said, "and I suspect Your Grace hasn't had any dinner."

Janeta gave a little cry.

"No dinner? Then you must have something at once."

"I am not hungry," the Duke said. "But I see, Jackson, you have thought of me as you did when I was a boy and you used to spoil me with tidbits from the Dining-Room table after the guests had finished."

"You needs something more substantial than a sandwich, Your Grace," Jackson said firmly. "Chef'll have something ready in half an hour."

"Very well," the Duke said good-humouredly, "if you insist?"

Her took a glass of champagne which had been poured out for him, and the footman put the plate of sandwiches down on a small table beside him.

Then, as the servants withdrew, he said to Janeta:

"You see I am well looked after in my Grandmother's house."

"They all love you," Janeta said with a little throb in her voice. "That is why I know why they could not bear anything . . . wrong to . . . happen to you."

The Duke drank half of his glass of champagne and put it down beside him.

Then he said:

"Because the people in this house feel like this, Janeta, we have got to save them from what I know will be to them an utter and complete disaster."

Her eyes were on his, but she did not interrupt and the Duke went on:

"I will explain what has happened from the beginning, and then I hope you will still want to help me."

"Of course I will!" Janeta said impulsively, then subsided into silence.

The Duke told her how he had arrived while her father was having breakfast and how Lord Brandon had been delighted when he said they wished to be married.

"I was just thinking," he went on, "we were out of the wood, when your stepmother came into the Breakfast-Room."

Janeta stiffened.

"So early," she murmured.

"She had heard I was in the house and was, of course, curious to find out what I wanted."

"What . . . did she . . . say?"

There was no doubt now there was a fear in Janeta's voice.

"She said," the Duke said slowly, "that in your father's absence she had given her consent to your marriage to Major Hodgson because you were both so much in love, and it would be impossible for you to behave so dishonourably as to change your mind because you wished to be a Duchess."

He told Janeta the truth because he thought it was

best for her to know what they were up against, and he was not surprised when she gave a cry like that of a small animal in pain.

Then she sprang to her feet, saying:

"I knew Stepmama would not let . . . me go. The only thing . . . I can do . . . is to disappear as I wished to in the . . . first place. Hide me! Please . . . hide me where she . . . cannot find me."

She stood in front of him and the Duke could see that her whole body was convulsed with fear.

Her eyes went from him towards the window as if she thought that by running out into the night it would be possible for her to escape.

The Duke was silent for what seemed a long time before he said:

"If you do that, and even if I helped you to hide where your Stepmother could not find you, that would still leave me unprotected and caught in the trap she has set for me."

The way he spoke made Janeta stare at him, and slowly, almost as if she did so against her will, she sat down again on the sofa.

"I have not told you before because I thought it unnecessary," the Duke said, "but now I want you to listen to the truth. Your Stepmother has made up her mind to marry me and she intends to tell your father to divorce her, citing me as the co-respondent."

He spoke quite unemotionally, but as he expected, Janeta stared at him as if she could hardly believe what she was hearing, and then her eyes dropped before his and she said incoherently:

"I . . . somehow thought . . . she might be . . . threatening you, but . . . not like . . . that."

She drew in her breath and then said:

"How can she be . . . so cruel to Papa . . . when he loves . . . her . . . and trusts her."

The Duke did not speak, and after a moment as if she were working it out for herself, Janeta said:

"Then if Papa . . . divorces her, does that mean that . . . you will . . . marry her?"

"To behave honourably and as a gentleman, I shall be forced to do so," the Duke said. "But let me say, Janeta, that now I understand what your Stepmother is like, and I realise that beneath her beautiful face she has the heart and soul of the devil. So I feel like saying that I would rather die than make her my wife!"

"I understand," Janeta said, "and as I feel the same about Major Hodgson, what can we do? Please tell me what we can do!"

"I have thought it out very carefully," the Duke replied, "and there is only one way we can save ourselves, although I am almost afraid to suggest it to you."

"If I can save you and myself, I will do anything . . . anything."

She gave a little shudder, which seemed to shake her whole body, before she added:

"How could I . . . marry a man like . . . Major Hodgson, and not go . . . mad with the . . . horror of it? How could you marry Stepmama and hurt all the people who believe in you?"

"Exactly," the Duke said, "and therefore we have to take what may seem to you a rather drastic step. But, as you have already said, anything is preferable to the fate that your Stepmother has planned for you."

There was a little pause before Janeta said in a very small voice:

"What do . . . we have . . . to do?"

"We have to be married at once," the Duke said quietly.

"Married?"

He knew as she spoke that this was something that had never occurred to her, and for a second she could not comprehend that he meant it.

"Why? How?" she faltered, and he went on:

"You must see it is the only possible solution, and I have made every arrangement. We shall be married first thing tomorrow morning and then leave immediately for Paris, where we will spend our honeymoon."

He paused before he continued:

"There will be nothing your father can do once the wedding has taken place, and by the time we return, both he and your Stepmother will have to accept the inevitable."

"But . . . but," Janeta murmured, "you . . . do not . . . want to . . . marry me."

"I do not think either of us wishes to be married," the Duke said, "especially in such unpleasant circumstances, but there is no alternative. I had actually been compelled to arrange with your father and Stepmother that I would take you back to Brandon House tomorrow at noon."

Janeta gave a little gasp and he went on:

"When I left, your Stepmother was arranging for Major Hodgson to come as well, so that your father could speak to you both."

His voice deepened as he went on:

"But I am absolutely convinced that however eloquently you might explain your dislike of him, your Stepmother would overrule your father and make him give, as she swore she already had, his blessing to your marriage."

Janeta shut her eyes before she said:

"She can always...twist Papa into saying and believing...anything she wants."

"Well, then," the Duke said, "the only thing we can do is to make sure that we do not only not arrive at Brandon House when they expect us, but have already left the country."

Janeta linked her thin fingers together before she said in a very small voice:

"If we...are married...I shall be your... wife."

"You will be my wife," the Duke said, "and I think you will find it a good deal preferable to being married to an old man who is cruel to his animals."

He could not suppress a somewhat cynical note in his voice. He was thinking that most women he knew would be overjoyed at the thought of becoming a Duchess and would certainly not look as worried and perturbed as Janeta.

"But I suppose," she said in a little above a whisper, "when...we are married...I do things...that upset you...and make mistakes...and you hate me. What can...we do then?"

The Duke smiled, and it made him look very attractive and beguiling.

"First of all, I will look after you, Janeta, so that you do not make many mistakes, and secondly, while we have to be married in this strange and desperate manner, I think we are both intelligent enough to try to make the very best of the situation in which we find ourselves."

He paused before he went on:

"I know it may not be easy, but I believe, since we share a number of interests, that we shall find we have a common ground on which to become good friends."

He thought as he spoke that he must sound rather pompous. At the same time, because Janeta was so young and so frightened, he knew that to be married to any man would be for her an alarming jump in the dark.

Because she did not speak, he continued:

"There are a lot of things I would like to show you in Paris, besides buying you a trousseau, which you can hardly ask your Stepmother to provide!"

Now there was a note of amusement in his voice as he felt he had made a joke, but Janeta did not smile and merely said:

"It is . . . humiliating for you to . . . have to marry me when I possess . . . nothing in the whole world but . . . the clothes I am wearing."

"On the contrary, I think it will be rather interesting to see if we can turn you from a very pretty schoolgirl into a sophisticated and beautiful lady of fashion," the Duke said.

He saw Janeta's surprise at his words and went on:

"Actually, I have already started my appointed task. One of the reasons why I am so late returning from London, apart from having to get a Special Licence from the Archbishop of Canterbury, whom fortunately I have known for some years, is that I have brought back with me a wedding-gown, a dress in which you can travel, and several others which will at least keep you clothed until we can visit the *haute couture* designers in Paris, who are famous all over the world."

As he spoke, and he was sure he was not mistaken, the colour came back into Janeta's pale cheeks and there was just a faint air of excitement about her.

Then she said:

"Are you quite sure . . . if we are . . . married as you say . . . Stepmama will not send my father . . . after us to bring me back . . . and perhaps charge you . . . for marrying me illegally . . . as I am a minor and did not have his approval."

"It is, of course, possible for him to do that," the Duke agreed, "but I am not being conceited, Janeta, when I say your father was ready to welcome me as a son-in-law as would a great number of other parents in the social world."

His voice was cynical as he finished:

"So I am quite sure he would not wish to make himself a laughing-stock by trying to annul a marriage which would be a social advantage to any girl."

"That is true," Janeta said, "and you do not think that Stepmama will be able to . . . stop us . . . before we get . . . away."

She looked around with frightened eyes as she spoke, as if she were almost expecting her stepmother to come into the room.

Once again she reminded the Duke of the spotted deer in the park, ready to flee at the first sight of a stranger.

"I am quite certain," he said soothingly, "that your

Stepmother will be expecting us to arrive, as I agreed, at noon tomorrow. What I am going to suggest now is that while I have something to eat, you go upstairs, unpack the clothes I have bought for you, and, if there are any alterations that are essential, get my Grandmother's housemaids to do them before tomorrow morning."

For the first time since his return Janeta gave him a little smile.

"How did you guess what would fit me?" she asked.

"I knew your height," the Duke said, "because your head is about four inches higher than my shoulder, and I explained to a dressmaker who is very famous in the fashion world how thin you were. Although she did not believe me, I was convinced in my own mind that I was very accurate in my calculations."

"I will be very embarrassed," Janeta said, "if, after all the trouble you have taken, the dresses turn out to be too small and I am fatter than you think."

The Duke laughed.

"You can only make sure of that by trying them on." He eyed her. "And I suspect they will fit fine. Now, go to bed, Janeta, and I will collect you from here at a quarter to nine tomorrow morning. We are being married in the Chapel at the Castle by my own Chaplain, and no one will know anything about it until we have crossed the Channel and are on the way to Paris."

"You are not going to tell your Grandmother?" Janeta enquired.

"It is too late tonight because she has retired," the

Duke replied, "and it will be too early for me to see her tomorrow morning. But I will write her a letter, and I know Grandmama will be intrigued and amused because she enjoys anything that is unusual, and will somehow stave off the curiosity of any other relatives when they read the announcement of our wedding in the newspapers."

Janeta had risen as he was speaking, and when he did so, too, she looked up at him and asked:

"Promise me . . . swear that by doing this . . . you will really . . . help yourself . . . as well as me."

"I assure you," the Duke replied, "there is no other possible way that I can be free of your Stepmother, just as I am quite sure there is no other way you can be free of Major Hodgson."

"Then thank you," Janeta said, "for being so kind, and I will try . . . if you will help me . . . to be a . . . good wife and not upset you or get in . . . your way."

"We will talk about that tomorrow," the Duke said. "Now, do as I say, Janeta, and try on the clothes, then go to bed. Try to sleep, for I want you as my wife to look so beautiful that those who do not know the real reason for our precipitate marriage will imagine it is because I find you irresistible and am afraid I may lose you if I do not make sure you belong to me."

He knew as he spoke she would respond by doing everything she could to look attractive for him.

As she left the room, Jackson announced his dinner was ready and he walked towards the Dining-Room.

The Duke thought with a faint smile on his lips

that all women were the same. They could not resist a challenge when it concerned their looks.

He was, however, not thinking so much of Janeta as of himself when he returned to the Castle to send for his Chaplain who lived in his own apartments at one end of the great building.

When he had given him his instructions as to what he required, he settled down at his desk to write to Lord Brandon.

When he sent for Mr. McMullen, it was to inform him that the letter was to be carried by a groom and delivered at Brandon House at exactly twelve o'clock and not one moment before.

The Duke had also written a letter to his Grandmother which he intended to deliver himself when he collected Janeta.

Then he told McMullen that the Chapel was to be decorated very early tomorrow morning with every white flower that was obtainable in the gardens and hot houses.

His secretary stared at him, and as it was impossible not to be aware of what he was asking him silently, the Duke said a little dryly:

"You are quite right, McMullen, I am being married, and I want you to be very tactful and diplomatic in dealing with all the numerous people who will beseige you with questions as to why the marriage has taken place."

"May I offer Your Grace my warmest congratulations," Mr. McMullen said, "and I imagine the lady in question is Miss Janeta Scott."

"You are quite right," the Duke replied.

"In which case," Mr. McMullen said smiling, "I

am confident that Your Grace will be very happy. I have barely spoken with Miss Scott myself, but Mrs. Robertson, the housekeeper, and the maids have all enthused over her beauty and find her one of the most pleasant young ladies who have been to the Castle."

The Duke was surprised.

He knew that his secretary was telling him the truth, for not only did Mr. McMullen never lie to him, but he never flattered him either and was often very blunt in his comments.

It had not struck him that while she seemed so thin, pale, and frightened, other people would think Janeta beautiful, but he supposed she did have an unusual beauty, even if it was not in what he thought was his taste.

Aloud he replied:

"Thank you, McMullen, and now I want you to send the announcement of my wedding to the newspapers and to tell everyone who enquires that it took place so speedily because my bride's parents thought she was too young to be married and I had no wish to wait and perhaps lose her in the process."

"In other words, it is an elopement, Your Grace."

"Exactly," the Duke agreed, "and make it sound as romantic as you can! It is what people might expect of me and will certainly offset anything unpleasant or derogatory that might be said about our behaviour."

"I understand exactly, Your Grace," Mr. McMullen said, "and once again, my congratulations."

When he left him, the Duke went to bed, but he

lay awake thinking this marriage would be very different from any he had ever envisaged.

He had always known that in his position he should marry someone whose blood was as good as his own, but he had also assumed that his bride's mother would be part of the social world which would expect a huge congregation of friends in the Church and an enormous reception afterwards.

There would also be a display of wedding-gifts which would, because he was a Duke, make one room resemble Aladdin's cave.

Instead of which there would be no spectators except his secretary at his wedding, and he would not be obliged to shake hands with over five hundred people and make a speech which because of the innuendos in previous speeches he would undoubtedly find embarrassing.

He told himself that under the circumstances that aspect of his marriage was a relief, and he could only hope that what followed would not be as difficult as might be expected.

'Because Janeta is very young,' he thought, 'I shall be able to teach her what to do, and once she has got used to being a Duchess, and has made friends of her own age, we can more or less live our own lives except when we appear in public.'

It sounded quite satisfactory, and yet the Duke deliberately forced away some questions which came to his mind.

He also had an uneasy feeling that Janeta would not be content, as any ordinary girl would be, merely with the social position he had given her as his wife.

He had the idea she would want more of life and perhaps more than he could give her.

Then he told himself he was being imaginative and the sooner he went to sleep the better.

As she dressed the following morning, Janeta could not help being excited.

To begin with, she had never imagined that she would ever possess anything so beautiful as the wedding-gown the Duke had bought her from London.

She was not really surprised that it fitted her almost perfectly.

She had already learnt he was so clever and so exceedingly well organised in everything he did that it was inevitable he should be able to guess her measurements down to the very last inch.

He had also given her a gown that she was sure had been part of the fairy tales she had told herself at the Convent.

Because her family ignored her and only occasionally did she hear from her father and never from any other relatives, she would tell herself stories in which the people who appeared in them time after time became very real.

Naturally, when she grew older and the other girls talked of what would happen when they were married, she found a Prince Charming in her dreams who she was sure now was exactly like the Duke.

Because it was in fact almost as if she had invented him herself, she knew he was the sort of man she admired.

He was accomplished as a rider and at every masculine sport, and was also kind, considerate, and to be relied on if things went wrong or her life was in danger.

Sometimes in her stories she would be captured by brigands or threatened by wild animals, or even, although she knew it was childish, goblins and gnomes.

But the Prince always rescued her in the nick of time, and she told herself as she dressed that that was exactly what the Duke was doing now.

He was rescuing her from an Ogre in the shape of her Stepmother, and when he carried her away on a magic carpet, it would be impossible for anyone ever to capture her again.

"You looks lovely, Miss, you do really," the housemaid who was helping her dress exclaimed.

Looking in the mirror, Janeta knew she had literally stepped into her own fairy-tale.

After the plain, schoolgirl clothes she had worn at the Convent, and which were all she had to put on when she had returned home, it was extraordinary how different she looked.

Her gown was of white gauze, sprinkled with diamanté like tiny dewdrops, and ornamented with frills caught with small bunches of orange blossom which echoed the wreath that was provided for her to wear over a long veil.

Janeta was not to know that the gown had been made and just finished by a Court dressmaker in Bond Street for a foreign Princess who had ordered it while she was in London, and which was to have been sent to Portugal the following day.

The Duke, however, by begging, cajoling, and bribing the dressmaker, with whom he had spent a lot of money in the past, had persuaded her to relinquish the gown and make another model of it at breakneck speed in time for the Princess.

He had also chosen a very pretty travelling-dress of deep blue satin which was the colour of Janeta's eyes and a cape over it edged with ermine, just in case it was cold crossing the Channel.

A small bonnet trimmed with blue ostrich feathers to match the gown completed the ensemble.

Although it was exorbitantly expensive, the Duke was thinking only that wearing these clothes, Janeta would look to those who saw her exactly as they would expect any bride of his to look.

He allowed the dressmaker to add several more gowns that were ready and, remembering that Janeta had nothing whatever with her, bought a collection of lingerie that was as he well knew the style of diaphanous elegance affected by the many women who had enticed him in the past when he opened their bedroom door.

To Janeta, after the austerity of her years at school, such garments were almost too lovely to be worn.

When she put on for the first time in her life a silk chemise trimmed with real lace and real silk stockings, she wondered how the Duke could be so knowledgeable about clothes that excited a woman.

"Now, sit down, Miss, while I fixes your veil," the maid was saying.

Looking at the mirror, Janeta stared at her reflection, thinking she was seeing someone she did not know and who undoubtedly was an illusion of her mind.

When she was told the Duke was waiting, she went slowly down the stairs with no-one to see her except old Jackson, two footmen, and the maids who had helped dress her.

As she did so, she felt as if she were leaving behind the world of loneliness and terror, stepping into a fairy story with a man who was different from any man she had ever seen before except in her dreams.

The Duke was looking exceedingly smart, and as he smiled at her, Janeta felt a strange sensation in her breast that she had never known before.

He took her hand and helped her down the steps to where his closed carriage was waiting, and before he shut them in, old Jackson said:

"God bless Your Grace, and you, Miss, and I knows you'll find happiness together for the rest of your lives."

"Thank you, Jackson," the Duke said.

The old man had spoken so sincerely that Janeta felt the tears come to her eyes and it was impossible for her to say anything.

'No-one will understand,' she thought as they drove away, 'that we are not an ordinary bridal couple very much in love with each other, but that is what the Duke wants people to think and I must behave as he wishes me to.'

The Duke bent forward to take from the small seat opposite them a bouquet of white flowers.

"These come from my own hot houses," he said.

"I had always hoped my bride would carry them on my wedding-day."

"They are very beautiful," Janeta managed to say, looking down at the star-shaped orchids.

"I brought the plants back with me when I returned from India," the Duke said. "One day I must tell you about them, because I am sure you will find many species in the conservatory are unusual and, I think, very beautiful."

"I . . . am sure . . . I shall," Janeta agreed.

She was perceptive enough to know he was talking ordinarily, as if to reassure her that nothing frightening was happening.

When they reached the Castle, she felt a moment of panic sweep over her in case she did the wrong thing.

'Suppose I fail him and he is angry with me,' she thought. 'Suppose after all Papa does follow us and denounces our marriage as being illegal.'

Then, as the servants ran down the steps over the red carpet to open the door, the Duke said:

"Welcome, Janeta, to your future home and, although our marriage is a very strange one, I hope we will somehow strive to find happiness together."

His voice was quiet, but his words were clear, and she had the feeling he had thought out his little speech as being the right thing to say to her in the circumstances.

She therefore smiled at him through her veil and he led her up the steps, through the Hall, along a wide corridor hung with pictures and ancient armour, before in the distance she heard the sound of an organ being played very softly.

The Chapel was in the oldest part of the Castle and the early morning sunshine was coming through the stained glass windows.

There was a profusion of white flowers and the fragrance of them combined with the music made it seem very beautiful to Janeta. She felt, too, although it was difficult to put into words, an atmosphere of sanctity.

She was sure those who prayed in the small place through the ages had left the vibrations of their faith behind.

At the same time, she was still afraid she was doing the wrong thing and that she would not be able to make the overwhelming man beside her happy.

As if he knew what she was feeling, the Duke, instead of taking her up the aisle on his arm, held her hand, and as her fingers trembled in his, she felt the warm strength of him moving into her body like a shaft of sunlight.

The Duke's Chaplain, who was an elderly man, was waiting for them in front of the altar, and as he started the Service, Janeta stole a glance at the Duke and thought he looked very grave, as if he were feeling this was a decisive and irrevocable moment in his life.

Almost passionately she prayed to God and her mother who was in Heaven to help her, and at the same time she knew that what lay ahead would not be easy.

Yet she must try with every nerve in her body and every thought in her mind to please the Duke after he had saved her from Major Hodgson and her Stepmother.

As she felt the ring go on her finger and heard the Duke's quiet, deep voice repeating after the Chaplain the words which made her his wife, she felt that no-one could be more lucky than she had been in not being forced to marry a man she loathed and from whom she shrank in terror.

Then she and the Duke knelt, and the Chaplain blessed them. As he did so, Janeta was certain she heard in the silence of the Chapel the voices of angels and her mother saying as she had said to her before she died:

"God is always with you, my darling, never doubt that. Trust in Him and you will always be safe."

She knew then it was her mother who through the Grace of God has saved her from taking her own life as she had intended to do, and had brought the Duke into her life when she had thought she was utterly alone and forsaken with no-one to whom she could turn for help.

"How can I ever be grateful enough?" she asked herself, and felt as they walked down the aisle that the angels were still singing.

She also felt an irrepressible surge of happiness because now that she was the Duchess of Wynchester no-one could hurt or frighten her anymore.

She wanted to tell the Duke what she felt, but there was no time. Instead, she hurried upstairs and changed into her travelling-dress.

Her beautiful white wedding-gown was packed into her trunk, and a quarter of an hour after the wedding they were moving down the drive in the Duke's travelling-chariot, drawn by six horses.

Janeta was very conscious of the Duke as he sat

beside her, and as she wondered what they should say, he said as he drew his watch from his breast pocket:

"It is nine forty-five, and we have exactly two and a quarter hours to be well out of reach before your father and Stepmother learn what we have done."

The way he spoke seemed to break the dream which had encompassed Janeta like a golden cloud since the moment she had put on her wedding-gown.

With difficulty she remembered that the Duke was not the Prince Charming with whom she was identifying him.

Instead, he was a man in the same predicament as herself, threatened by a cruel, vengeful woman, who would rage with fury when she realised what had happened.

Impulsively, because she was frightened, Janeta put out her hand and slipped it into the Duke's.

"You are quite sure," she asked, "Stepmama will not . . . be able to . . . find us in . . . Paris?"

"If she does, what can she do about it?" the Duke asked lightly. "We have won, Janeta, we have defeated her!"

There was a note of elation in his voice that Janeta found irresistible.

"We have defeated her," she repeated.

Yet, as she tried to feel as pleased as he was, she had an uneasy qualm in case her Stepmother did not acknowledge they were the victors.

chapter five

By the time they reached Folkestone, Janeta was very tired.

Because it was a cross-country journey, it had been impossible to do it by train, and they therefore travelled by road, changing horses at posting-houses.

As the Duke regularly made the journey there from Wynchester Castle, they were his own horses, so naturally the journey had been done in almost record time.

Nevertheless, when she saw the Duke's yacht moored at the Quayside, Janeta was glad the journey was over.

It had been impossible at the speed they were travelling to talk very much, and she had, in fact, slept a little. She suspected the Duke dozed, too, even though when she woke she always found his eyes open.

They went immediately aboard the yacht, a new acquisition of which he was very proud. Every modern gadget was incorporated in the vessel, and everything looked very spic and span.

But Janeta was glad to go to her cabin and, at the Duke's suggestion, undress and get into bed.

"When we get to Paris," he said, "I will, of course, engage a lady's-maid for you, but until then I am afraid you will have to look after yourself."

Janeta laughed.

"That is something I have done all my life, so it will be no imposition!" she replied.

Then she wondered if always having a lady's-maid would be somewhat restrictive and if actually she would prefer to manage on her own.

The Steward brought her dinner on a tray and told her that the Duke was eating a good meal upstairs.

"As soon as His Grace has finished, we'll be moving out of harbour. The sea's smooth and I don't think Your Grace'll find it unpleasant."

"I am sure I will not," Janeta replied.

She knew, because her father had told her, that in ships Stewards waited on ladies even in their cabins. She had expected to find it embarrassing, but the Steward who had brought her dinner was a middle-aged man with a sunburnt face and a twinkle in his eyes.

Janeta did not feel the least shy that she was sitting back against the pillows in a frilly pink bedjacket over a diaphanous nightgown which the Duke had bought her in London.

In fact, because it was all so different from what she had ever experienced, she felt it was unreal and talked to the Steward quite naturally as he took her tray away.

Then, as she was thinking she would now be able to sleep, the Duke came into her cabin.

She smiled at him as she said:

"I have been told you have eaten a good dinner, and I can well believe it, because the food is delicious."

"I chose my Chef with great care," the Duke replied.

He sat down on the side of the bed and asked:

"How are you? Not too tired I hope."

"I thought I should be too excited to be tired," Janeta replied, "but now I feel the lap of the waves will soon rock me to sleep."

She spoke without sounding the least affected, and after a moment the Duke said:

"I am afraid this must seem very strange for a wedding-night and not the least what you expected yours would be like."

To his surprise Janeta gave a little cry.

"I know from what you are ... saying," she replied, "that I should have dined with you! To be truthful I had ... forgotten it was our ... wedding-night, and was only thinking with relief that we had ... escaped from Stepmama and that once your beautiful yacht had left harbour, there would be no chance of her or Papa ... stopping us from leaving England."

For a moment the Duke was surprised, then he thought with amusement that Janeta was certainly unpredictable and different from any other woman he had ever known.

He could not imagine that any of the ladies to whom he had paid attention in the past would have forgotten for one second that she was a bride and he was her bridegroom.

The wedding-night would have meant something very special, and he would have been expected to play his part with ardour.

For a moment it flashed through his mind that, in spite of the decision he had made about it, it might be better to suggest to Janeta there and now that they should from the start lead a normal married life.

Then he knew that it would certainly frighten her and she might look at him with the same fear in her eyes that had been there when he first saw her.

"She is so young," he told himself, "that I must move slowly and not do anything disturbing until she accepts me as a friend and someone she can trust."

He therefore said:

"You are quite safe now. I promise that neither of us will be disturbed until we reach France, and I am sure your father will not think it worthwhile pursuing us to Paris."

Janeta took a deep breath.

"Then we are . . . free," she said, "and that is why I am feeling . . . happy."

"I want you to feel happy," the Duke said. "Ever since we met, you have been frightened and agitated, which is something I shall dislike very much if it continues."

"I am not . . . frightened . . . anymore."

The Duke rose from where he was sitting.

"Then I will leave you to go to sleep," he said, "and when you wake up, we shall be able to continue our journey without any worries to spoil what I hope will be a very happy honeymoon."

"I am sure it will be," Janeta said, "and thank you more than I can ever say for bringing me here and making sure that Stepmama has no longer . . . any authority over . . . me."

Her voice had deepened over the last words, and then she asked:

"That is true, is it not? Now I am your wife, no-one can order me about or make me do things that frighten me."

"No-one except me!"

He had the feeling as he spoke that he wanted to draw Janeta's attention to himself and was not prepared for her to give a little laugh as she said:

"You are much too kind and understanding ever to be an Ogre like Stepmama, and if you give me an order, I shall want to obey it."

"That is a step in the right direction," the Duke said, smiling, "and what every woman should feel where her husband is concerned."

"You should have told me," Janeta said in a low voice, "that I ought to have dined with you tonight. It was thoughtless of me to let you dine alone."

"You were tired after the long journey," the Duke said, "and I think, quite frankly, it would have been very unflattering and rather humiliating for me to find my bride yawning and perhaps even falling asleep while I talked to her."

Janeta gave him a quick glance in case he was being serious and not teasing her as she thought he was, and then she said:

"I will make up for it on any other night. But I am more afraid, since you are used to lovely ladies who are sophisticated and, I am sure, very witty, that it is you who will be yawning, not me."

"The only answer to that," the Duke said, "is that we must wait and see. Go to sleep, Janeta, and just remember we have both been very clever and have outwitted the enemy."

"I hope you are right," Janeta said in a soft voice. Then she added:

"Goodnight my very kind, clever husband to whom I am very grateful."

She was obviously not expecting him to kiss her, and the Duke went from the cabin, closing the door behind him.

He went up on deck to watch the Captain take the yacht out of harbour. He thought, in the fading light with the last glow of the sunset vivid in the sky, that the world was a very much happier place than it had been for the last two days.

He still found it hard to realise that he had escaped from the trap that Olive had set for him, in which had it not been for a miracle in the shape of Janeta's unexpected appearance, he would have been helpless and totally unable to extricate himself.

He had the uneasy feeling as he thought of her that it would not always be plain-sailing in the future when they returned to England.

He refused, however, to let these thoughts depress him. He went down to his own cabin thinking, as he

got into the comfortable bed that he had chosen especially for his yacht, that his only problem now was
how to make Janeta happy and make quite sure her
Stepmother did not intrude on her.

However, even as he assured Janeta that they had
cleverly found a way of escape, he knew that in
Olive they both had an unpredictable enemy who he
suspected would, in some way he could not envis-
age, seek revenge upon them.

"Damn it! I am being over-imaginative," the Duke
told himself before he fell asleep. "It is quite impossible for her to do anything now. All we have to do is
keep out of her way, even though it will mean Janeta
not seeing her father."

They travelled by train to Paris and arrived there late
in the evening.

This time Janeta was not tired but excited, and
when they drove from the *Gard du Nord*, she sat
forward on the edge of the carriage-seat so that she
could look out of the window at the tall grey houses
with their shutters.

She also saw, moving about the Boulevards under
the gaslights, people who looked, she told the Duke,
exactly as she thought the French would look.

"What do you mean by that?" he enquired.

"Very smart, very jolly, and very much alive," she
replied.

He thought it was an amusing and apt description.
He was to find in the next two or three days that
Janeta had an original way of describing everything

they saw which was different from what he had expected.

Because she had been incarcerated in a Convent for the last four years and she had told him they were very strictly secluded in it with practically no contact with the world outside, he had thought she would be astonished at a great many things they saw and perhaps even shocked by them.

Instead, she found the beauty of Paris enthralled her. The Duke realised she watched the smartly dressed women and the elegant men as if they were part of a stage show and had no relation to ordinary life.

On their arrival Janeta had been thrilled with the Duke's house which he had actually bought only two years previously, and which was situated on the *Champs-Élyseés*.

It had belonged to a French aristocrat who had been forced for economic reasons to retire to his Château in the country and had offered it to the Duke lock, stock, and barrel.

"Only you, Wynchester," he had said, "are rich enough both to pay the price I require and also to appreciate the treasures that have over the centuries been accumulated by my ancestors."

The Duke had enjoyed the compliment and had not hesitated, knowing it was a fine house and its contents exceptional.

He told himself, at the time, it was exactly what he wanted for himself when he visited Paris, which he did frequently.

It was also a place where he could enjoy his *affaires de coeur* without being afraid that the servants would carry stories to the lady's husband, or that he would be the victim of spiteful gossips who were to be found everywhere in London.

He had actually played with the idea, although he did not like to think of it now, of taking Olive to Paris for the weekend when Lord Brandon was in Scotland.

He had, however, decided it was too arduous a journey for such a short visit, and had not mentioned it to her.

He was glad now that her presence would not haunt the beautiful rooms hung with tapestry and pictures by celebrated French artists.

Also, he had no qualms about installing Janeta in the exquisite Louis XIV bedroom, with its painted ceiling of Venus rising from the waves.

"It is a dream house," Janeta cried as they sat down for a late dinner.

The Chef excelled himself, and Janeta said as they finished:

"That was a meal that might have been served on Olympus."

The Duke smiled at the enthusiasm in her voice.

"Are you suggesting we are one with the gods?" he enquired.

"Of course!" Janeta replied. "How could you be anything else? Do not forget they were always coming down from Olympus to enjoy the delights of human beings, and, of course, to bemuse and bewilder them."

"Are you suggesting that is what I have done to you?" the Duke asked.

Janeta put her elbows on the table, and he thought

107

as she did so that she was looking exceedingly attractive in a gown he had bought for her in London.

He had a feeling, however, that something was missing and he was suddenly aware that she was wearing no jewellery.

He had never thought of it because every woman with whom he had associated in the past had always glittered like a chandelier. He now thought it was rather remiss of him not to have been aware that being so young and unimportant, Janeta possessed no jewellery of any sort.

Then he saw she was considering him with her large blue eyes, almost as if he were impersonal—perhaps one of the pictures on the wall.

"What are you thinking?" he asked.

"I am trying to put into words what . . . I feel about . . . you."

"You have already told me that I am kind and understanding."

"You are both those things to me," she said, "but I was . . . thinking of you as a . . . man and I think it is . . . only now I realise how . . . exceptional you . . . are."

The Duke raised his eyebrows but did not interrupt as she went on:

"I can understand why women fall . . . in love with you and why men admire you for all the . . . things you have done and for being so proficient at sport, but I think there is much more to you than . . . that."

"In what way?" the Duke enquired.

"It is difficult to describe a magnetic personality in words, which often convey an unintended meaning. I am sure you have found already that you are a born leader, but I think perhaps you are not using that . . . leadership in quite the . . . right way."

The Duke was astounded before he said:

"I do not understand. You must explain what you are saying."

"That is what I am trying to do," Janeta answered, "and perhaps, because I am not of your world, I see things . . . differently from the . . . way your friends would."

The Duke waited and she went on:

"As I have said, you lead people and they admire you for your achievements, but I think you do not realise, or nobody has told you about it, that you could lead in a very different way."

"I cannot understand," the Duke insisted. "What are you suggesting?"

"The Greeks, whose gods we were just talking about," Janeta replied, "led the world in thought, and that is where I am sure you are needed at this present time."

The Duke, still bewildered and astonished, said:

"I find what you are saying very extraordinary, Janeta. In what way do you believe I could lead the world in thought, as you put it?"

She made a little gesture with her hands before she said:

"That is what I am trying to put into words. Perhaps it is politics, perhaps something deeper and more fundamental, but I cannot help feeling because you are so outstanding, so much bigger than the average person, that is where you are needed."

The Duke sat back in his chair.

"How can you possibly say things like that when

you know so little of the world and have spent the last four years of your life in a convent?" he asked.

"It may seem almost impertinent," Janeta said, "but since it was a French Convent, they constantly discussed politics and the world situation. Although they approached it from entirely a religious angle, I could understand what what was lacking in France, in England, and I expect in other countries, was the leadership which comes, not from Priests, but from personalities."

She gave him a shy little smile and added:

"From people like yourself who could alter the world because they are in a position to do so."

The Duke thought that never in his life had anyone spoken to him in quite this way, and yet he did not pretend to misunderstand what Janeta was saying.

He was only absolutely astonished she should say it, and he thought not in his wildest imagination would he have expected a conversation like this, on his first night in Paris.

The next day was very different.

Before Janeta was awake, he had sent for many of the top couturiers, knowing that when it came to the King of them all, Frederick Worth, they would have to go to him.

In the meantime the Duke ordered so many things he thought Janeta required that she protested that it was too much.

"No woman ever has too many clothes," he replied.

"Then I am an exception," Janeta insisted. "Please, you have given me so many things already

110

that I am overwhelmed. What is more, I shall never have time to wear them!"

The Duke laughed.

"In a few months, perhaps sooner, you will be telling me you have not got anything to wear, and will think I am mean if I do not spend the same amount of money all over again."

Actually, he was finding it very amusing to notice the difference clothes made to Janeta.

He soon realised, even without the help of the French Couturiers, what colours suited her best, and while he thought her lamentably thin, the French admired her body and thought it was exactly the right shape to show off the *dernier cri*.

Although Janeta found the silks, satins, chiffons, velvets, lace, ribbons, and flowers were all alluring, she was relieved, when having been given an enormous order, the Couturiers left, volubly expressing their thanks.

"Now let us go out in the fresh air," the Duke said. "I will take you to luncheon in the Bois."

They drove there in his Chaise, and he thought Janeta in her elegant gown of leaf green was as attractive as the trees under which they sat.

Now the serious mood she had shown him the night before had vanished, and she chattered away like a child, asking questions about the trees, the people, the restaurant, and anything else that caught her fancy.

Her natural laughter, the Duke thought, was infectious, and he had never known a woman who was so unselfconscious about herself or her appearance.

'She is very young,' he found himself thinking.

At the same time, if he were honest, he would have to admit he had enjoyed every moment of their luncheon and had not, as he had half-expected, been in the least bored.

It was only when they encountered two French friends that he was aware from the eloquent compliments they paid Janeta that they found her exceedingly lovely.

When the Duke introduced her as his wife, they were astonished.

"I had no idea you were married, Your Grace," one of the men said. "In fact, we were talking about you only a night or so ago and someone quoted you as being the most eligible bachelor in the whole of Great Britain."

"Now I am a married man," the Duke smiled, "and actually my wife and I are here on our honeymoon."

After that they were overwhelmed with congratulations and good wishes, and one of the Frenchmen, whose bold eyes made Janeta feel a little embarrassed, insisted that they repair to his sister's house to tell her the good news.

His sister was a *Contesse*, and the way she greeted the Duke and the manner in which she looked into his eyes and her hands lingered in his told Janeta that she had been, at one time, if not still was, important in his life.

The *Contesse* was exceedingly pretty, with the *chic* of a Parisienne and a way of expressing herself with her eyes, her hands, and her lips which was different from anything Janeta had seen before.

She watched her and told herself that was what the

Duke wanted from someone whom he found attractive, but she was not certain it was something he would like in his wife.

Because the *Contesse* was so sophisticated, Janeta suddenly felt very gauche and ignorant, a schoolgirl who knew nothing of the world in which the Duke shone so brilliantly.

It struck her that if her Stepmother had behaved the same way as the *Contesse* was behaving, that was what he found attractive but was obviously lamentably lacking in herself.

As they drove back from the *Contesse*'s house, the Duke said:

"You are very quiet. What are you thinking?"

Janeta did not answer, and he said after a moment:

"Tell me. I think it is a mistake to have secrets from each other."

He was speaking half jokingly, but Janeta answered:

"Perhaps it can be a mistake to be too frank. A man might prefer a woman to be mysterious so that it would make him curious."

The Duke realised why she was saying such things and he took her hand in his. Now her fingers were not fluttering as before when she had been so frightened.

But he felt a little tremor go through her and wondered if it was because he was touching her.

Then he said:

"I think, Janeta, that you thought the *Contesse*'s manner was very French and it was something you should emulate yourself. That would be a great mistake."

"Why," Janeta asked.

"Because one of the things which is most delightful about you is that you are natural. You do not pretend. You are not, as you have just put it, mysterious."

"But, perhaps," Janeta said, "you will find that very dull."

"Does it matter to you what I feel about you?" the Duke asked.

"Of course it does," she replied. "If we have to be together because we are married and you much prefer women to behave as the *Contesse* did just now, then I will try, but I do not think I would be very successful."

"I think it would be a disaster," the Duke replied. "What I find most interesting about you, Janeta, is that you talk to me naturally and unaffectedly, and tell me, I hope, everything that is in your mind and heart. That is what I find interesting, because it is not an artificial act put on to attract and enslave any man who happens to be present."

Janeta gave a little sigh.

"That makes things much easier," she said, "and thank you for telling me."

"I would like to add," the Duke said, "that the *Contesse* is very French, and I have always been determined that my wife—when I had one—should be very English."

Janeta gave a little laugh before she said:

"I feel I have a . . . chance at any rate . . . being as you wish . . . your wife to be."

She took her hand from the Duke's as she spoke, and then the next minute was laughing at some children running about in the gardens of the *Champs-Élyseés* with balloons that were getting loose and floating up into the trees.

The Duke took Janeta to various restaurants which he thought would amuse her, and invariably in the largest and most popular ones he met friends, who were astonished to learn of his marriage.

Finally, after they had been several days in Paris, an announcement appeared in the French newspapers copied from the English.

The Duke showed to Janeta what had been printed. She was silent for a long moment before she said:

"I suppose Papa and Stepmama will know by . . . now where . . . we are."

"I imagine so," the Duke replied. "That is why I think we should now go farther South, and I thought if it pleased you, we would pick up the yacht again at Marseilles and come home by sea."

Janeta was delighted. She enjoyed Paris, but at the same time she was acutely conscious, whatever the Duke might say, of the difference between her and his French women friends whom they met whenever they went out.

Once they were back on the yacht she felt very much more at ease.

Although the idea that she was jealous never crossed her mind, she admitted liking to be alone with him and made every effort to talk about things that interested him and on which he could instruct her.

It was, however, very rough coming back through the Bay of Biscay, and despite the fact that she was a good sailor, the continual movement gave Janeta a headache, and she was glad to go to bed, if only to save herself from sliding from one side of the cabin to the other.

It was quite late at night when the Duke came down from the Bridge and, seeing her light still on, came into her cabin.

"Are you all right?" he asked.

"Yes, quite," Janeta said. "Unless you think we are going to the bottom."

"Do not dare insult my ship!" the Duke replied. "She is behaving magnificently, and the Captain and crew are delighted with her."

"I feel safer in bed." Janeta said, then smiled.

As she spoke she looked so attractive in the light from a lantern that the Duke found the words "I think I shall join you" trembling on his lips.

Then he realised that the way she was looking at him was that of an admiring younger sister.

There was not a glint of coquetry in her eyes, and she smiled at his wind-swept hair and had obviously noticed that his tie was somewhat awry.

It was again with the affection and perhaps admiration of a schoolgirl for her big brother.

The Duke noticed that, with the excellent food they had been eating in France and her freedom from fear, Janeta's face had filled out a little and her skin seemed to glow with the translucence of good health, and her eyes sparkled in the same way.

With her strange silver-threaded hair falling over her shoulders, she looked, he thought, like a Siren luring Ulysses to his doom, and the Duke had for the first time a desire to kiss her and to find out what her reaction to it would be.

He almost reached out his hand towards her, but he was afraid of seeing her large eyes contorted with fear and of damaging what he knew was already a warm companionship that excluded any embarrassment.

"Are you looking forward to going home?" he asked abruptly.

"It will be exciting to be back at the Castle," Janeta replied, "but I think more than anything else I am longing to ride your horses."

"I shall enjoy riding with you," the Duke said, "and I have a great deal to show you."

There was a still silence, and then he added:

"When we get home, we will have a lot of things to talk about because, as I am sure you are aware, Janeta, our lives will be very different from what we have enjoyed this past week in Paris."

Janeta gave a little sigh.

"I suppose there will be many demands upon you, and, of course, if you go to London, they will expect you to appear at Buckingham Palace and at Marlborough House."

"You have obviously been thinking it out," the Duke said. "We will also have to face the music of being married and you will have to take your place as my wife."

"You promised you will not let me make any . . . mistakes," Janeta said quickly.

"I will certainly keep that promise," the Duke said. "And you must remember that from the point of view of the world, we married because we were very

117

much in love with each other, and that was the reason for such haste."

"I am not quite . . . certain," Janeta said slowly, "how one . . . pretends to be . . . in love so that people . . . notice it."

The Duke thought that the real answer to that was to be in love and for him to make love to his wife.

But he found it a very difficult thing to put into words.

Instead, after a rather pregnant silence he said:

"We shall just have to see what happens. I am sure, once we are at the Castle or in London, we shall do what is right by instinct."

Janeta looked worried.

"It may be easy for you," she said, "but it is very much more difficult for me, since I really do not know what your friends will expect or how I should behave when they are there."

"We have three more days before we reach home," the Duke said. "Let us forget this knotty problem for the moment, and when the sea is calmer we will talk about it."

"That is a very good idea," Janeta agreed, "and I am sure you ought to go to bed. The wind, if nothing else, is very tiring."

"That is true," the Duke said absent-mindedly.

Once again he was thinking how attractive Janeta looked, and that her lips as she smiled at him were very young and, as he knew, untouched and unspoilt.

'If I kissed her,' he thought, 'it would be like kissing a flower or touching the petals of a rose.'

There was a little flicker inside him at the thought. Then Janeta snuggled down amongst the pillows.

"I am going to sleep," she said, "and I hope in the morning the storm will have abated a little. If nothing else, the noise of the wind and the incessant creaking are very tiring."

"You are quite right," the Duke agreed, "and we can only hope for calmer seas ahead."

He rose as he spoke and moved unsteadily across the cabin to the door.

It was quite an effort to negotiate his way through it and, as he shut it behind him, Janeta closed her eyes and started to say her prayers.

chapter six

As they drove down the road to Wynchester Castle, the Duke thought with a feeling of intense satisfaction that he was home.

He had not forgotten those awful moments when he had thought that, thanks to Olive, he would have to give up the Castle, the five thousand acres he owned round it, and live abroad with a woman whom he knew now he would have hated more and more every moment of their married life.

"I have been lucky! More lucky than I can say," he told himself, "and I am very, very grateful."

The Castle in the sunshine looked exceedingly

beautiful, with the windows gleaming a welcome and his standard flying on the roof against the blue sky.

Because it all moved him so intensely, he said to Janeta:

"This is your home for the future and I hope you will grow to love it as much as I do."

"It is very lovely," Janeta said in a small voice, "but very . . . large."

He knew she was feeling frightened of finding herself alone in such a huge building, and he replied lightly:

"I shall be with you, and I expect also an inordinate number of my relatives, who always expect the Castle to provide them with free board and lodging at any moment they require it."

Janeta gave a little laugh, which had been the object of his last remark, and when he drove up to the front door, he felt that she was not as tense or as nervous as he had feared.

Because he had been eager to arrive home driving his own horses, they had taken a train from Folkestone, where they had left the yacht to the nearest main-line station. Here the Duke's Phaeton was waiting with two outriders to escort them on their journey home.

He thought Janeta appreciated the style in which they were travelling, though she did not say anything. He did not want to ask her for compliments, but for her to express them naturally.

Now, as they walked into the Great Hall of the Castle and she saw the flags hanging on either side of the mediaeval fireplace and the ornate carved staircase with the portraits of the Duke's ancestors hanging above it, she made a little sound of awe and admiration that he appreciated.

They were late in arriving, and after the Duke had insisted that Janeta have a small glass of champagne to wipe away the fatigue of the journey, he escorted her upstairs to the exquisite bedroom which was always occupied by the Duchesses of Wynchester.

He knew, without her saying anything, how much she admired the painted ceiling, the brocade panels each of which contained an appropriate picture, and the furniture, which was French.

The carved gilt mirrors were as unique as the canopied bed, which was also carved with cupids and doves.

"As I know you must be tired after such a long journey," the Duke said, "I suggest you put on something comfortable, like a negligee. We are not dining downstairs, but in your private Sitting-Room next door."

He then left her with Mrs. Robertson, the housekeeper, who had already unpacked some of Janeta's trunks which had gone ahead of them from the station in a brake pulled by six horses.

"We're very excited to welcome you home, Your Grace," Mrs. Robertson said. "Tomorrow you'll find there's a mountain of presents awaiting downstairs in the Ball-Room."

"Presents?" Janeta questioned.

"Yes, Your Grace, they've been pouring in ever since the announcement of your marriage in the newspapers. His Grace's very popular, as I 'pect you knows."

Janeta thought, though she did not say so, that all

the presents would be for the Duke. It would be surprising if there was even one for her personally.

She did not want to think at the moment about her likely reception by the Duke's relatives and friends, but only to try to get accustomed to the Castle and to realise she was the mistress of it.

Because she had been so terrified when the Duke had brought her here from London, she had not taken in any of her surroundings but had been concerned only with a feverish anxiety to get away from her Stepmother.

Now she felt as if a little voice throbbed inside her mind saying: "This is yours! Yours! Yours! This is where you will be safe for ever!"

In the warm scented bath which Mrs. Robertson prepared for her she felt as if her troubles vanished. The Duke, as he had promised, would protect her, even though she was back in England and within reach of her Father and her Stepmother.

"They cannot touch me now," she told herself.

She hardly noticed when Mrs. Robertson dressed her first in a diaphanous nightgown in a very soft shade of blue and then in an exquisite satin and lace negligee which matched it.

When she had arranged Janeta's hair, she said:

"His Grace's waiting next door and I'm sure he'll think, as I do, that Your Grace looks very beautiful."

She had been so deep in her thoughts that Janeta had hardly noticed her reflection in the mirror.

Now she looked at herself she thought she looked her best, though she wondered if the Duke would think she could be compared with the lovely women who had fawned on him in Paris.

Then because she wanted to be with him, she thanked Mrs. Robertson and hurried across the room to the communicating door which the Housekeeper opened for her.

The Duke was standing in front of the mantelpiece in the Sitting-Room, and as she entered, Janeta gave a little gasp.

The whole room was decorated with white flowers, and great bowls of Madonna lilies stood on each side of the fireplace and on side-tables of carved gilt. There were garlands over every picture and a mass of star-shaped orchids covered the top of the mantelpiece.

Janeta clasped her hands together and exclaimed:

"How pretty! Did you do . . . this for . . . me?"

"For my wife," the Duke replied, "and I also have a wedding-present for you, Janeta."

As he spoke, he took a velvet-covered box from an adjacent table and opened it. Inside there was an exquisite necklace of flowers made in diamonds.

"Shall I put it on for you?" he asked.

"It is lovely! Perfectly lovely!" Janeta exclaimed. "But you should not have . . . given it to . . . me."

"I realised in Paris," the Duke answered, "that you had no jewellery. I should, of course, have brought some of the family jewellery for you to wear, but this is your own, Janeta, and belongs to you."

As he spoke, he put it round her neck and fastened the clasp at the back.

As he did so, his fingers touched her bare skin and she felt a strange little quiver like a thrill run through her.

It happened so quickly that it was gone even before she could savour it. Then the Duke said:

"I have another present and one which I should have given you as soon as we were married, but I wanted to buy it from my own Jeweller in England, who knows my taste exactly."

As he spoke, he opened another very much smaller box which Janeta had not noticed and took from it a diamond ring.

"This is your engagement ring," he said, "and I hope when you wear it, you will forget that we never had a proper engagement."

He was smiling as he put it on her finger, then he realised that Janeta was looking worried.

"What is troubling you?" he asked. "I hoped you would be pleased by my gifts."

"They are magnificent and wonderful," Janeta replied. "But I feel it is wrong for you to give me anything so valuable."

"Wrong?" the Duke questioned.

"You see, I am embarrassed by your generosity," Janeta explained, "because I have nothing to give you in return."

There was a little silence and the Duke deliberated whether he should tell her what she could give him. At the same time, he feared that if he did so, it would be too soon and would frighten her.

While he hesitated, the door opened and the servants came in with the dinner.

Two footmen carried first a small table already laid, and were followed by the Butler with champagne. Again the Duke insisted that Janeta should have a little.

He told her it was because he did not wish her to be tired, but she knew perceptively it was really because he hoped it would sweep away her fear of the Castle and of coming home to England.

When they sat down at the table, the Duke set out to amuse Janeta in the same way as he had when they were in Paris.

But now he talked of his home, the mischief he had got into as a small boy, and various secret places in the garden and on the Estate which he wished to show her, as he had made them peculiarly his own.

He also spoke of the old retainers she would meet and of the horses which he was waiting for her to ride.

It all sounded so entrancing that Janeta listened to him with her eyes shining and a transparent happiness which made her look very different from the terrified, miserable girl he had brought first to the Castle and through whom he had found a way of escape from the trap set for him by her Stepmother.

They finished their dinner with dessert consisting of huge peaches and grapes from the Duke's hot houses, which seemed to Janeta also symbolic of the perfection she found in everything that concerned him.

Then Jackson came to the table with a decanter in his hand.

"Port, Your Grace?" he asked.

The Duke shook his head.

"No, thank you, Jackson, I have had an excellent dinner, and when I have finished my glass of champagne, I shall not want anything more."

"Excuse me, My Lord," Jackson said, "but this is

a very special wedding-present with which I was entrusted soon after Your Grace left for France. I was given instructions that you were to drink it the first night Your Grace returned home to celebrate your home-coming and your marriage."

The Duke looked interested.

"A very kind thought," he said. "Who was the donor?"

There was a little pause before Jackson answered:

"I asked the same question, Your Grace, and was told it came from someone who admired Your Grace enormously and wanted to extend to you his good wishes."

"And his name?" the Duke insisted.

"The Groom who brought it wouldn't tell me that," Jackson replied, "but as it happened, Your Grace, I recognised his livery."

The Duke smiled.

"You always had a sharp eye, Jackson! Who was it who wished to be so mysterious?"

"The livery, My Lord, was that of Lord Brandon."

There was a little silence, and thinking the Duke's answer was now in the affirmative, Jackson filled a small wine glass by his side with port, put the decanter on the table, and left the room.

Supposing this must be an olive branch from Janeta's father, the Duke picked up the glass of port.

Then as he lifted it to his lips Janeta gave a cry:

"No! No! Please! Please!" she begged. "Do . . . not drink . . . it."

She spoke in such an agitated way that the Duke looked at her in surprise.

"Why not?" he asked.

"Because I feel . . . in fact . . . I know, it will be . . . dangerous. I am sure it was not Papa who sent you the port, but . . . Stepmama."

"Do you think it will make me ill?" the Duke asked with a faint twist to his lips.

"I think," Janeta said in a very low voice, "it might . . . kill you!"

The Duke looked at her in astonishment, then put down the glass as he said:

"Why should you say that? I cannot believe that, however angry your Stepmother may be with you and me, she would risk being accused as a murderess."

There was silence for a moment, then Janeta said:

"I will tell you something very strange that happened the first day I returned home from school."

The Duke was listening as she went on in a low voice:

"Papa and Stepmama were in the country and I went straight there. I found most of the old servants who had been in the house when I left, and they were pleased to see me. But there was one new man."

She paused before she continued:

"He was the first footman who, I realised as soon as I arrived, was very much in my Stepmother's good books. She praised Henry—that was his name—and kept asking him to do things for her and made, in a way, a fuss of him which seemed to me rather . . . unusual and . . . undignified."

She stopped speaking, and twisted her hands:

"Someone else new was the youngest housemaid, who was allotted to look after me. Because Emily was a pretty, attractive girl and rather nervous, I talked to her and she told me she had only just arrived in the house and had been brought there by Henry, as they came from the same village.

"The next morning, when she was dressing me, Emily told me secretly, as if she could not bear to keep it any longer to herself, that she and Henry were engaged.

"'I'm ever so happy, Miss,' she said, 'except that Her Ladyship seems to have taken a dislike to me. I've a feeling that I shan't be allowed to stay here.'

"I was sorry for the young girl," Janeta went on, "because I knew only too well that if my Stepmother had taken a dislike to her, she was doomed."

The Duke was listening, and at the same time, he was wondering how this concerned the port that Janeta had warned him not to drink.

Then after a little pause Janeta continued:

"Later that day I went unexpectedly into the Drawing-Room and found Stepmama having what was obviously an argument with Henry. They were both talking in low voices, so I could not hear what they said.

"When I appeared, Stepmama walked away, but I knew by the way her eyes were flashing and the hard line of her mouth that she was angry. Henry, red in the face and obviously upset, hurried from the room."

"How old was the man?" the Duke interposed.

"Oh, between twenty-five and twenty-seven, I suppose," Janeta replied. "He was good-looking and more refined than most of the other footmen."

"Go on," the Duke said.

"I did not see Emily again that day until I went

upstairs to dress for dinner. As soon as she appeared, I realised she had been crying.

"'What is the matter, Emily,' I asked.

"'It's Her Ladyship, Miss Janeta,' she replied. 'She's been complaining about me to the Housekeeper, and Henry thinks, and so do I, that I am bound to be dismissed when we're paid our wages at the end of the week.'

"'I am sorry, Emily,' I said. 'I wish I could help you.'

"'Nobody can help me,' Emily said miserably. 'I was so happy to come here to be with Henry and I've done my best, I have really, Miss.'

"She looked so pathetic as she spoke," Janeta said, "that I put my arms round her, saying:

"'Cheer up, Emily, perhaps you will have another chance.'

"As I spoke," she continued, "the door of my bedroom opened and Stepmama came in.

"'There you are, Emily!' she exclaimed.

"I felt Emily stiffen as she moved away from me and dropped Stepmama a little curtsy.

"'I have just been saying that you look run down and a little tired,' Stepmama went on in such a kind manner that I looked at her in surprise.

"Emily was surprised, too, and she said:

"'I've done my best, M'Lady, I have really.'

"'I am sure you have,' Stepmama said, 'and I realise it is a lot of work when we have people staying in the house, and, of course, you have not really got accustomed to the hours.'

"Again," Janeta said, "she was being so pleasant, I could hardly believe it.

"Then Stepmama went on:

"'I have brought you, Emily, a tonic that I know will make you feel much better. It is one I always take myself, which makes me feel on top of the world. Take a small wineglass full of it when you go to bed, and I know it will make you much stronger and able to continue working hard, as I know you wish to do.'

"As she spoke," Janeta said, "she handed Emily a medicine bottle and then left the room, telling me to hurry or I would be late for dinner.

"'There you are Emily,' I said jubilantly, 'it was not as bad as you expected, and I have never known my stepmother to be so kind!'

"'Very kind, Miss,' Emily agreed. 'I'll do exactly as she says and perhaps everything'll be all right.'"

Janeta stopped speaking and after a moment the Duke asked:

"What happened?"

"In the morning," Janeta said very quickly, "Emily was . . . dead!"

"Dead!" the Duke exclaimed. "I do not believe it!"

"It is true. She was found dead in bed and, when the Doctor came, he said she had died of a heart-attack."

"He did not suspect anything else?"

"No! He was very definite in saying her heart was affected and she must have died in her sleep."

The Duke was silent for a moment and then he said:

"Is that the truth?"

"I said to Stepmama," Janeta replied, "because I could not help it:

"'You do not think, Stepmama, that perhaps the tonic you gave Emily was too strong, and affected her heart?'"

"What did she reply," the Duke asked curiously.

"Stepmama looked at me in a way that always frightened me, and answered:

"'What tonic? I do not know what you are talking about!'

"'The tonic you gave Emily when you came to my room.' I replied.

"'I think you must be going mad!' Stepmama retorted. 'I would not have thought of giving that tiresome, idiotic girl anything, except her notice. If you ask me, that she has died is the best thing that could have happened. We are well rid of her.'

"She went from the room as she spoke, but I think Henry knew the truth."

"Why do you think that?" the Duke asked.

"Because he left without saying anything to anyone. The Butler reported to Papa that Henry had gone. Papa thought it was due to grief at losing Emily. But I was sure it was because he was too frightened to accuse Stepmama of being a murderess, which was what she had been."

The Duke put his hand up to his forehead.

"I can hardly believe that what you have told me is the truth!"

"It is, I promise you," Janeta said. "So please do not touch that port and tell Jackson to throw it away."

"After what you have told me," the Duke said, "though I cannot really credit your Stepmother would be so diabolical, I will certainly give my orders to Jackson."

He rang the bell as he spoke, and when Jackson came into the room, he said:

"You can take away the table, and, Jackson, the port is corked, or else it has been kept too long. Pour it away yourself and no-one is to drink it. Do you understand?"

"I understands, Your Grace," Jackson said. "I'll see no-one touches it."

He picked up the decanter as he spoke. The footmen carried the table from the room, and as they shut the door, Janeta gave a little sigh of relief and went to the window.

The sun was sinking in a blaze of glory behind the trees in the park. The last flicker of crimson and gold in the sky was reflected on the lake, and overhead the first evening star could be seen glittering faintly.

It was very quiet and very beautiful.

Because he knew Janeta had been upset by what had occurred at dinner, the Duke said:

"Tomorrow we will ride through the Park and I will take you to a flat piece of ground, where we can gallop our horses."

"I would like that," Janeta said. "But I have not ridden for some years, and I only hope that you will not be disappointed in me as an equestrian."

"I will teach you to ride," the Duke said, "as I am prepared to teach you a great number of things, and I promise, Janeta, it will amuse me very much to have such a willing and intelligent pupil."

"It will be very exciting for me," Janeta said. "But will you promise me that if I do bore you, and you think I am a nuisance, you will say so and perhaps find someone else to instruct me."

"It is a promise I can give you quite easily," the Duke said, "because I know it is something that will not happen."

He paused for a moment, and then he said:

"Amongst all the many different things I have done in my life, I have never taught anyone anything as far as I can remember, except my troopers when I was in the Army for a short time, and I suppose when I had a fag at Eton, I taught him his duties."

"I hope I shall be as bright as they were," Janeta said, smiling, and he said:

"My only concern is that I shall have to polish up my brain to keep up with you on a great many subjects. But at least I shall have the satisfaction of starting off as the Master."

"I think you will always be . . . that," Janeta said in a low voice.

She looked up at the Duke as she spoke, and her eyes were held by the expression in his.

She had no idea how lovely she looked in the fading light or that the glittering diamond necklace round her neck accentuated the whiteness of her skin and made the Duke aware of the soft curves of her breasts beneath it.

He drew in his breath, and then behind them the door of the Sitting-Room crashed open and Jackson exclaimed:

"Please, Your Grace, come at once!"

"What is it?" the Duke asked.

Then because he had never known Jackson to lose his pontifical calm, he hurried across the room, and following the elderly Butler, shut the door behind him.

Alone, Janeta stared after them and then, with a little murmur of fear, covered her face with her hands.

Outside in the passage the Duke said:

"What is it, Jackson? What is all this commotion?"

"I wants Your Grace to come with me," Jackson answered. "I've never known anything like it! Never in all m'born days!"

He hurried ahead of the Duke, who followed him to the small pantry which on the other side of the corridor was used for meals when they were carried upstairs.

As they entered it, the Duke saw one of the footmen lying on the floor and the other very pale in the face bending over him.

He stood up as the Duke appeared, and then as the Duke went down on one knee to examine the prostrate young man, Jackson said:

"I left James in here, Your Grace, for just two minutes while I went with Arthur to superintend what was left of the dishes served at dinner, returning them by the lift down to the kitchens."

The Duke knew that this was the usual procedure and was hardly listening.

Undoing the footman's waistcoat, he inserted his hand onto his chest. His heart had stopped beating and there was no doubt that the man was dead.

The Duke confirmed what he already knew by trying to feel for his pulse, and then he asked in a voice that did not sound like his own:

"What do you think happened?"

"I have no idea, Your Grace. No idea at all!" Jackson replied. "One moment he was standing here stacking the plates, and when Arthur and I comes back a few seconds later, he was down on the floor as you sees him—dead!"

It was then that the Duke saw that against the wainscot lay a wine glass.

He recognised it as the one that had been by his side at dinner when Jackson had filled it with port, and he knew as he looked at it that it could have easily rolled there from the footman's hand as he fell.

Getting to his feet, he glanced round the pantry and saw the decanter which Jackson had carried into the Sitting-Room was standing at the side of the sink.

He knew it would be a mistake to draw attention to it, so instead he said:

"I suggest, Jackson, you go to the stables and ask a Groom to ride into the village to request Dr. Graham to come here as soon as possible."

He turned to the footman and said:

"And you, Arthur, ask Mrs. Robertson for a sheet with which we can cover this poor boy and also a pillow for his head. Otherwise he is not to be moved. Do you understand?"

"I understands, Your Grace."

Jackson and the footman hurried away and the Duke, taking the stopper out of the decanter, poured the contents down the sink.

As he did so, he knew that if Janeta had not saved him, it would have been he who was lying on the floor instead of the footman.

He waited in a state of great agitation until Mrs.

Robertson arrived. When he had instructed her to wait until the Doctor came and not to move the dead man, he then went slowly back to the Sitting-Room, wondering, as he went, how he would tell Janeta what had occurred.

He knew it would greatly upset her, and he thought it was diabolical that this should have happened the first night that they had returned home, when he wanted her to feel happy.

He opened the door of the Sitting-Room and saw that Janeta was standing, as he had left her, beside the window.

Now it was growing dark, but it was not so dark that she could not see his face.

Before he could speak, before he could begin to put into words what he had to tell her, she gave a cry and ran across the room to throw herself against him.

"She . . . meant to . . . kill you! I know she meant to . . . kill you! Suppose you had . . . died! Oh, God, how . . . could . . . this have . . . happened?"

Her voice was almost incoherent because she had burst into tears as she spoke.

Then, as his arms went round her, she looked up at him, and in the dying light of the sun he thought that with her huge eyes swimming with tears, her lips parted, her whole body trembling against him, he had never seen anyone so lovely.

Without thinking, without wondering how he could comfort her, his lips came down on hers and held her captive.

For a moment he felt her whole body stiffen in astonishment, and then she seemed to melt against him as if it were all the protection and comfort she needed.

Because her lips were exactly as he had expected them to be, very soft, young, and innocent, he held her closer, and as he kissed her, he found awakening in himself sensations he had never felt before.

It was not the violent, fiery passion he had known with so many other women and which ended as quickly as it was ignited.

This was different. So different that for a moment he could hardly believe that what Janeta was making him feel was love. Then he knew that if he were truthful, he had loved her for a long time.

He had told himself she was so young that although she might not attract or amuse him as more sophisticated women had done in the past, he would protect and treat her with every propriety as his wife.

Now he knew he wanted a great deal more.

He wanted her love. He wanted to know that because she could arouse an indescribable rapture in him, he could arouse the same sensations in her.

It was not entirely physical. Yet because she was so lovely, so soft, and so unspoilt, he wanted her as a woman.

At the same time, he knew what she was awakening in him, and his whole body throbbed and thrilled in a way he had never known before in an ecstasy that was truly spiritual.

It made him know what he had found in Janeta was what had always been missing in the other women to whom he had made love.

The emotions they had felt for him and which he had imagined he felt for them had been very earthly, the natural desire of a body for a body, and nothing else.

Now he had an almost intolerable desire not only for Janeta's body, which already seemed a part of his own, but for her heart and for her soul.

Because she made him feel breathless, he raised his head for a moment.

He felt his whole being vibrate towards her, and he knew by the way she instinctively moved a little closer to him, and by the brilliance of her eyes, she felt the same.

"I love you," he said, and his voice was very deep and unsteady.

Then he was kissing her again, kissing her with long, demanding, passionate kisses which Janeta felt drew her heart from her body and made it his.

She had never guessed, never had any idea that anything could be so wonderful as the Duke's kisses.

She knew now that instinctively it was what she must have wanted from him, but had never envisaged it possible that he might love her.

Yet because they had been so happy together in Paris, and because she had felt safe and protected even when they had reached England, she had loved him without knowing it.

"How can I have been so stupid as not to know that what I felt was love?" she asked herself. "Yet could I have imagined that love would be like this?"

She felt his lips become more insistent, more demanding, and something very strange and exciting leapt within her.

She wanted to give him what he wanted, although she was not certain what it was. She knew only that she was in a strange Heaven, where everything was so thrilling, so poignant, it was unreal.

'If I died at this moment, I should have known perfection,' she thought.

Then she knew that she did not want to die; she wanted to live, she wanted to be with the Duke.

She wanted him to kiss her and go on kissing her, and for them to be closer, even closer than they were at the moment.

Only when he kissed her until she felt she had reached the zenith of happiness that was almost unbearable did she give a little murmur and hide her face against his neck.

"My darling, my sweet," the Duke said. "How could you make me feel like this? How can I love you as I never knew I was capable of loving anyone?"

"I love . . . you," Janeta whispered. "I have loved you for a . . . long time . . . but I did not know it was . . . love."

"I adore you," the Duke said. "My darling, once again you have saved me from a trap set by your Stepmother."

Janeta raised her face to look up at him. Her eyes were very wide and frightened as he said:

"The port was poisoned!"

"How do you know for certain?"

"It has killed one of the footmen who drank from the glass that Jackson poured out for me and which you prevented me from drinking."

"Oh, no!" Janeta exclaimed in horror.

"There is nothing I can do," the Duke said. "But

to save a scandal I only hope the Doctor will think it was a heart-attack."

Janeta shut her eyes for a moment and then she said:

"It might . . . have been . . . you, and then I would have . . . died too. How can we . . . live knowing that Stepmama will . . . try again?"

The Duke pulled her so close against him that she found it difficult to breathe, and then she said:

"I am frightened! Oh, darling . . . wonderful Hugo, I am . . . frightened that I shall . . . lose you!"

Her voice broke as she hid her face against his shoulder.

The Duke lifted her up in his arms and carried her across the Sitting-Room into the bedroom. He set her down on her feet beside the bed and took off first her diamond necklace, throwing it casually on the bedside table, then undid her negligee and, while she was still crying, lifted her onto the bed.

She gave a little murmur because she did not wish to leave him, but as she was still crying, it was impossible for her to speak.

The Duke went to the door and locked it, and a few seconds later he slipped into bed and gently pulled Janeta into his arms.

She gave a little gasp of surprise, but she did not say anything. He knew she had now stopped crying.

The Duke held her very close and then he said:

"Now, listen, my darling, you have got to be very clever and sensible about this. We have managed to save ourselves, or rather you have saved me, up to now. We cannot allow your Stepmother to defeat us or to make our lives the Hell she intends."

"She meant to . . . kill you," Janeta said in a whisper. "Then I would be . . . back in her power and she would punish me."

"Whether I live or die," the Duke said, "I will make certain you are not dependent on your Father or your Stepmother. But that is immaterial, because I intend to live and I intend my adorable little wife to be very happy with me."

His arms tightened as he went on:

"So let us think for a moment not of the abominable scheming of your Stepmother, but that we have found each other and that I love you."

"Do you . . . really love me?" Janeta asked.

"I love you as I have never been in love in my whole life before."

To make sure she was convinced, he drew her a little closer as he went on:

"I am not pretending there have not been a great number of women in my life. But what I felt for them was the quite natural passion any normal man feels for a beautiful woman who makes it obvious that she is attracted by him."

He felt Janeta give a little shiver as if she were shocked, and he continued:

"But the feelings they evoked in me were very different from the feelings I have for you."

"How can they be . . . different?" Janeta said.

"It is hard to put into words," the Duke answered. "At first I just wanted to protect you and save you from yourself. Then you crept into my heart, and I know it would be impossible for me to contemplate my life without you beside me, without your helping me, stimulating my mind and inspiring me."

His lips touched her forehead before he went on:

"This is something I have never said to another woman, because they did not mean anything more to me than a pleasure and an amusement which was very expendable."

His cheek was against hers as he said, his voice very deep:

"I have no wish to live without you. I want you with me by day and by night, and even if you are not there, you will always be in my thoughts."

Janeta put her hand against his cheek before she said:

"I cannot . . . believe that you are saying . . . this to me. I love you until you . . . fill my whole world . . . the sea . . . and the sky! There is only . . . you, and you are so . . . wonderful in every way that I thought when we returned to England I was no longer . . . frightened of . . . Stepmama."

"You will not be frightened of her," the Duke said. "She is an evil that we have to fight. A Dragon which I, as your Knight, fortified by your love, will have to destroy."

He spoke as if he challenged the Devil himself, and for a moment Janeta felt a strange elation sweep through her as if she listened to a trumpet-call of courage. Then she said:

"How can we . . . always be on our . . . guard? What else can she do to . . . destroy you and how can we . . . anticipate it?"

The Duke drew in his breath before he said:

"Because I love you so much, my darling, I know the answer and it is a very strange one for me to give. The fact is I am convinced the God who has watched over us so far will not fail us in the future. We must have faith. We must trust in a Power greater than ourselves, and I think we will find a way out of this mess."

Janeta gave a little cry:

"Only you could say anything so wonderful! Only you could be so different from what anyone would expect. Oh, Hugo, I love you . . . I love you . . . I want to . . . be with you . . . I want to be . . . your wife. I want to give you sons and daughters to live in this marvellous Castle. I am only . . . frightened I am asking . . . too much."

"What you are asking is that I should live," the Duke said, "and please God, that is what I shall be able to do."

He kissed Janeta as he spoke, and for a moment his lips were not passionate and compelling. It was a kiss of dedication. The kiss of a man who vows himself to crusade against evil.

Then as he felt her move nearer to him, as he felt the softness of her body against his, he felt himself pulsating once again with that strange awareness of a love that was different.

"I love you, my precious darling," he said. "I could not bear to do anything to frighten you more than you are frightened already."

"You could never frighten me," Janeta said. "I am only frightened for you! I love you with every breath I draw, and every time you kiss me it is like being taken up to Heaven and I know that our love is . . . Divine."

She was unable to finish what she was saying because the Duke's lips were on hers and his hand was touching her, his lips holding her captive and his heart beating against hers.

He carried her up into the sky, and as she touched the stars and felt the light from them glitter within her and knew that they glittered, too, within the Duke, they became one.

Together they had found the Love of God which is Divine and all-powerful, against which no evil can prevail.

chapter seven

THE Duke woke with a feeling of extreme happiness.

He lay for some moments with his eyes closed and then was aware when he opened them that it was very early in the morning, and the sun was only just beginning to peep through the sides of the curtains.

He turned on his side to look at Janeta, and thought that with her strangely coloured hair spread over the pillow and her eyelashes dark against her cheeks, she looked very lovely, young, and vulnerable.

'I will look after and protect her for the rest of my life,' he thought.

Then like a dark cloud spreading across the sun, he remembered Olive.

Very quietly he slipped out of bed and left the room without waking his wife.

He knew he wanted to be alone to think, and to plan, if it were possible, what he could do for their safety.

He dressed swiftly without the help of his valet and went downstairs, where the first housemaids were coming on duty, and walked to the stables.

The sleepy Groom who emerged yawning from one of the stalls became more alert when he saw his Master and hurriedly saddled one of his spirited horses.

Then the Duke was off, riding across the Park, feeling the cool wind on his face and all the time thinking frantically of what he could do to protect himself and Janeta.

He had ridden for nearly an hour before he turned around to come home, and riding through a wood on the outskirts of the Park, he found a small gypsy encampment.

He recognised them as gypsies who came to the Castle every year and who, being Romanies, had his permission to camp where they wished.

For a moment as he appeared they stiffened and turned the rather hostile look they had for strangers towards him.

Then, when they saw who he was, their faces broke into smiles.

The Duke moved nearer to them and saw with interest that in the centre of the circle made by their caravans was the most magnificent stallion he had ever seen.

Pure white, without a touch of colour on it, the

horse stood proudly with an arched neck, which made the Duke think he had Arab blood in him.

As he reached the gypsies, their Chief came towards him to say:

"Mornin' Yer Grace. We're grateful once again fer Yer Grace's 'ospitality."

"It is nice to see you, Buckland. That is a very fine horse you have there."

"Very fine to look at, Yer Grace," the Chief replied, "but Oi'm contemplatin' 'ow Oi can destroy it."

"Destroy it!" the Duke exclaimed. "What do you mean by that?"

"Oi means, Yer Grace, this 'orse be th' devil's spawn an' not fit to live."

The Duke was so interested that he dismounted from his own horse, gave it to a gypsy boy to hold, and walked over to the stallion.

It was true he had never seen a finer or more magnificent animal, and when he patted its neck, the horse did not seem to mind but stood proudly, as if completely unaffected by what was happening around him.

"For Heaven's sake! Why should you wish to destroy such an outstanding creature?" the Duke asked.

"He's a killer, Yer Grace," the gypsy replied simply. "Oi were told when Oi was given 'im that he's killed three men an' injured several others. But like Yer Grace, Oi didn't believe it."

"Surely he needs only better training," the Duke said.

"No, Yer Grace, nothin' can be done with an animal that 'as the temperament of th' devil 'imself, as this one 'as! Me son rode 'im an' very nearly lost 'is life in doin' so. Another of our lads 'as got a broken leg, and 'twere fortunate it was not 'is neck!"

"I can hardly believe it!" the Duke exclaimed.

"Oi tells Yer Grace that it's the devil in 'im that makes 'im behave as he does."

"How does he behave?"

"When someone rides 'im, Yer Grace, 'e behaves perfect, then suddenly for no reason 'e goes mad. No human being can keep mounted on 'im when 'e 'as a kind of frenzy. It's not only frightening to behold, but as Oi've just said, no more men shall die 'cause of 'im."

"I can understand that," the Duke said.

At the back of his mind he was thinking that he had heard there were stallions that were peculiar in just this way, and that no amount of training could do anything to them, especially when they had grown to maturity.

Then, as he turned away, having no wish to see the death of anything so magnificent, an idea came to him.

It was almost as if the Power of which he had spoken to Janeta was guiding and helping him.

Slowly, because he was thinking it out, he said:

"I will buy that horse from you, Buckland."

The gypsy shook his head.

"No, Yer Grace, Oi wouldn't wish after all yer kindness to know Oi were instrumental in causin' yer death or leavin' ye crippled."

"Thank you for thinking of me," the Duke said quietly, "but I will not ride the horse myself, that I promise you. I am going to send the horse up to London to someone who will be interested in it."

"Well, that's different, Yer Grace," the gypsy answered.

"There is only one thing I would ask of you," the Duke said, "that one of your lads should lead it to the place in London where I wish it taken. I will, of course, pay him for doing so."

The gypsy thought it over.

"Luke's come to no harm," he said, "if 'e took the horse on a leading rein which 'e could let go of if 'e 'ad one of 'is turns."

"Exactly," the Duke agreed. "I will go back to the house and get a letter, which I wish you to deliver with the stallion, and also fifty pounds, which I will pay you for him."

He saw the gypsy's eyes light up, knowing it was a lot of money for a horse he had been about to destroy.

The Duke hastily mounted his own animal and rode back to the Castle. When he reached the front door, a Groom was waiting for him and he told him not to take his horse to the stables.

Then, running up the steps, the Duke went to his Study, where he sat down at his desk and knew once again, as if he were asking for guidance, what he should write to Olive.

He had remembered while he was talking to the gypsy that the next day she was to appear in a pageant in Hyde Park, which was being given in honour of the Queen's Birthday.

He took up his pen, and the words flowed almost as if they were being dictated.

My Dear Olive,

My wife and I were deeply touched when we arrived home last night to find your very special present waiting for us. It was too late then to enjoy it, but sometime today I am sure we shall be able to drink to our future happiness as you wished, and to you at the same time.

I feel one present deserves another, and I am therefore sending you a horse which, when you have seen him, I know you will wish to ride tomorrow, when you appear in the celebrations for Her Majesty's Birthday, and I can confidently say that no-one could look more beautiful on a stallion that might have been especially bred for you.

Once again my grateful thanks for your kind thought.

I remain, as ever,

Hugo.

He did not trouble to read the letter through, feeling as if every word of it had been spoken into his mind.

Then he put it into an envelope and addressed it to Lady Brandon, and inserted that in yet a larger envelope which he addressed:

Miss Smith,

c/o Lady Brandon,

Brandon House,

Park Lane.

It was the way Olive had instructed him to write to her secretly when they were having their *affaire de coeur* and even at the time he had thought cynically that quite a number of men must have had the same instructions.

Opening the safe which he had in his Study, he extracted fifty pounds in notes and ten gold sovereigns, which he put into his pocket.

Then he rode back to the gypsy encampment, gave Buckland first the money, then the letter, with instructions that his son was to deliver the stallion to the groom in the mews behind Brandon House in Park Lane.

He also told him to make sure when the boy did so, that the letter was taken immediately into the house.

Luke was overcome with the Duke's generosity in giving him ten sovereigns for his trouble and the gypsy Chief thanked him again and again for buying the horse.

"We'll be movin' off, Yer Grace," he added, "as soon as Luke returns, an' we be wishin' Yer Grace, an' yer new wife, happiness, a long life, an' a large number of sons to follow ye!"

"Thank you, Buckland." the Duke said, "That is what I am praying that I will have."

He rode home and found, as he expected, that Janeta was awake and missing him.

They had breakfast together in the Sitting-Room where they had dined, and the Duke thought in the morning sunshine his wife looked even lovelier than she had the night before.

"Why did you not tell me you were going riding?" she asked a little reproachfully. "I would have come with you."

"I wanted you to rest," he replied, "and I have every intention that we will ride together later in the day."

His eyes were on her face as he asked very softly:

"Did I make you happy last night?"

She looked at him, and he saw the answer in her eyes before she said:

"So happy . . . that I feel I must have . . . been dreaming. Why did no-one tell me that . . . love was so . . . wonderful and so . . . perfect that I still feel I am . . . flying in the sky."

"With me, I hope," the Duke said. "If I knew you were flying alone, I should be very frightened in case I lost you."

"Oh, Hugo," Janeta said impulsively, "I love you so much. I did not know that any man could be so gentle and at the same time so . . . strong and . . . exciting."

"I wanted to excite you, my beautiful wife," the Duke said, "and I am only afraid of frightening you so that, as nervous as the spotted deer in the Park, you run away from me."

"I will never . . . never do . . . that!" Janeta said with a note of passion in her voice. "I do not want to leave you ever, for a moment of the day or . . . night!"

The Duke knew as she spoke she was thinking of the Sword of Damocles which in the shape of Olive hung over their heads.

He wanted to reassure her that some instinct within him told him all would be well, but at the same time he knew that if his plan were successful, she must never learn that he had instigated it.

Because it was so much easier not to have to put his feelings into words, he pulled her up from the breakfast-table and took her to the window looking out over the Park.

"Today," he said quietly, "we are going to explore the places I told you about last night. Because I will not share you, my lovely one, with anyone, if anyone calls who wishes to see us, Jackson will be instructed to send them away."

"That is what I wanted you to say."

She moved nearer to him as she spoke, and as his arms went around her, he thought the softness of her body, which he could feel through the negligee she was wearing, was so alluring that he could feel the blood throbbing in his temples and a fire flickering inside him.

Then he told himself because she was so young and this was all new to her, he must be very controlled and, as he had been last night, very gentle.

He kissed her and tried hard not to make it a very passionate kiss before he said:

"Go and dress, my lovely one, and I will order our horses to be round in half an hour."

"Then I must hurry!" she said with a little cry of delight.

As she ran from the Sitting-Room to her bedroom, the Duke turned again to look out over the Park.

He hardly saw the sun flickering through thick leaves of the old oak trees and glittering dazzlingly on the lake.

Instead, he was praying as he had not prayed since he was a small boy, fervently, with almost a child-like belief that his prayer would be answered.

They had what was to Janeta an entrancing day, which had a fairy-like quality about it.

The Duke showed her the magic pool in the woods which was supposed to be haunted by nymphs. Then there was a tree, at the top of which the Estate carpenter had built him a look-out so that he could see for many miles over the land he owned.

They visited not only the woods, but rode beside the silver stream which fed the lake and saw the small fish darting in the clear water over the pebbled bottom, and to Janeta's delight they disturbed a king-fisher.

It was not only lovely, but she had the Duke beside her and she could see the love in his eyes.

Instinctively, when their hands went out to touch each other, their vibrations were joined, and it was almost as if once again he were making her his.

They had luncheon on the outskirts of the Duke's estate at a small black and white Inn, where the Inn-keeper welcomed them with delight.

They ate home-cured ham, cheese with bread that

came fresh from the oven, and drank home-brewed cider.

It was when they were riding back home that Janeta said with a sigh:

"How can I bear that . . . today should come to an . . . end."

The Duke knew what she was really saying was that perhaps there would be no tomorrow, but he replied lightly:

"There will be a lot more days like it, my darling, and even better ones."

"If only I could be . . . sure of . . . that," Janeta whispered, and he knew once again she was afraid.

Because he did not want her to think of anything but their happiness, when he took her back to the Castle, he insisted that she should rest before dinner.

When she protested, saying:

"I do not want you to leave me!" his eyes twinkled as he replied:

"Who said anything about my leaving you?"

Janeta drew in her breath.

"Oh, darling, wonderful Hugo, why did I not think of that! Then of course we must rest."

She hurried up to her bedroom, and when the Duke joined her, the sunblinds were drawn a little because the evening sun was dazzling, and beneath the curtains of the cupid-canopied bed, Janeta looked very small and insubstantial.

Yet she was so utterly desirable that the Duke knew that never again in his life would he see any other woman's face but hers.

They had dinner once again in the Sitting-Room because, as the Duke said, they were still on their honeymoon. Only when they took up their social duties
would they have to conform to behaving in a tradi-
tional manner.

"I love having you to myself," Janeta said. "It is
so much easier to talk when there are no servants in
the room, except when they bring in the courses, and
we have only the flowers to listen to us, and their
fragrance to make us feel romantic."

"I can feel romantic with you without flowers,"
the Duke said.

"I feel the same," Janeta said. "Oh, Hugo, Hugo,
how lucky we are, and I treasure every moment,
every second we are together!"

She spoke with a passionate intensity, but the
Duke knew without her saying anything that she eyed
the food suspiciously when they were served with a
fresh salmon, and drew in her breath when Jackson
offered him Claret.

Because he knew it would be impossible for Olive
to poison wine which was in his own cellar, the Duke
insisted on drinking only an excellent vintage which
he had brought back from France the previous year.

At the same time, he was well aware that Janeta
was trying to disguise her fear from him, but that
almost every mouthful he ate made her nervous.

"We cannot go on like this!" he told himself. They
had another night to go through before he would
know if the present he had sent Olive had been effec-
tive, or had misfired like the one she had sent them.

Mr. McMullen had informed him, when Janeta was not there, that the Doctor had diagnosed the footman's collapse as a severe heart-attack.

"He said it was strange, Your Grace," Mr. McMullen had relayed, "because he knew James's family so well, and there was, in fact, no-one among his parents or brothers and sisters who had disturbances of any sort with their hearts."

The Duke had little to say on the matter. He merely told Mr. McMullen to send a large wreath to James's funeral, and to make sure the family receives his condolences and the promise that as soon as they had another son old enough to take James's place, he would be welcomed at the Castle.

There was nothing else he could do, and he had no intention of talking about it to Janeta.

The only way to keep her happy and unafraid was to carry her away on the rapture of love into the fairy-land they had discovered last night.

As it was something he wanted ardently himself, it was not difficult, when dinner was over, to kiss her until it was impossible for either of them to think of anything else except love.

It was a long night but a very happy one, and only when the Duke awoke early, as he had done the morning before, was there an expression of anxiety in his grey eyes.

As he looked at his sleeping wife, he knew that like the Knight she believed him to be, he had confronted the Dragon, only it would be some hours yet before he knew whether his onslaught had been successful.

Once again he went early to the stables, and riding

the same way as he had the day before, came to the wood where the gypsies had encamped.

Now there was no sign of them, except the ashes of their fire in the clearing and the wheel marks of their caravans.

Just for a moment in the quietness the Duke wondered if he had dreamt the whole episode and if the magnificent white stallion had just been a figment of his imagination.

Then as if he must know the truth, he galloped back to the Castle.

Mr. McMullen had made arrangements that when the Duke was in residence, a Groom should fetch the newspapers from the nearby station, so that if the train was on time, they usually arrived about nine o'clock.

When he got back to the Castle, the Duke did not go upstairs but into his Study, knowing that his Secretary would bring in the newspapers as soon as they arrived.

It was only a few minutes after nine when Mr. McMullen came into the room. He carried three newspapers in his hand and before he put them down in front of the Duke, he said:

"I am afraid, Your Grace, I bring bad news."

"Bad news?" the Duke asked sharply, thinking for one terrifying moment that something might have happened to Janeta.

"Yes, Your Grace," Mr. McMullen replied. "There has been an accident to Lady Brandon. It is on the front page of both *The Times* and *The Morning Post*."

The Duke did not speak, but took the newspapers

160

from his Secretary and saw that in both newspapers there were headlines regarding the celebrations for the Queen's Birthday in Hyde Park.

Then a little lower down he read:

There was unfortunately one tragedy during the afternoon. Lady Brandon, a famous Society beauty, led twelve of the finest horsewomen in England onto the ground dressed as previous Queens of England. Lady Brandon herself was arrayed as Queen Elizabeth, then Her Majesty addressed her troops as they prepared to confront the Spanish Armada.

A noted horsewoman, Lady Brandon was riding a magnificent white stallion which outshone every other horse ridden by the ladies accompanying her.

They paraded amidst great applause from the crowd into the centre of the arena, but then tragedy struck.

Something must have upset or frightened the white stallion, because he galloped wildly away, scattering spectators as he did so, and made a crazy effort to jump the six-foot spiked iron fence which cordoned off that part of the ground.

He failed to clear it, impaling himself for a few seconds on the spike at the top until, as he fell, he flung Lady Brandon to the ground, breaking her neck.

Her Ladyship died instantly, and the horse, having broken a leg, was eventually destroyed.

It is with deepest regret we report this tragic

end to a famous hostess and the wife of a distinguished Statesman.

Lord Brandon . . .

The Duke did not need to read any more, which he knew would be a description of the posts Lord Brandon had held and the honours he had received in his long life.

He put down the paper, aware that Mr. McMullen had watched him read it.

"I can only offer my condolences, Your Grace," he said quietly.

"Thank you, McMullen," the Duke said. "Take away the newspapers and destroy them."

"Destroy them?" Mr. McMullen asked, obviously startled by the order.

"I do not wish Her Grace to see them at the moment," the Duke said. "It will upset her, and I want to choose my moment when I tell her what has happened to her Stepmother."

"Of course, I understand," Mr. McMullen replied. "The papers shall be destroyed before anyone else in the house sees them."

"Thank you," the Duke said. "I know I can rely on you not to speak of this to anyone."

He gave a deep sigh, as if a heavy burden had been lifted from his shoulders, then he went up the stairs two at a time towards Janeta's room.

He opened the door quietly and found that she was not awake but was sleeping peacefully.

He stood looking at her for a long moment, thinking that he loved her overwhelmingly and that now

162

their situation was very different from what it had been previously.

He went into his own room and started to undress, realising as he did so there was no hurry. There was no longer that terrifying feeling that the sands were running out and any moment might be his or Janeta's last.

They were safe—free from the menacing fear of being assassinated. Free from the danger of an evil woman who had been determined to destroy them.

The Duke stood for a moment at the window and thought the sun had never been so bright or so gold, and then he went back into his wife's room.

As he got into bed beside her, he thought once again there was no hurry to tell her what had occurred, and no fear to make them cling to each other frantically in case the next moment was their last.

He put his arms around Janeta and she gave a little murmur of happiness and moved closer to him.

"It may be cruel of me to wake you up," the Duke said gently, "but I want to kiss you and tell you how much I love you."

She opened her eyes, and he saw the radiance on her face.

"That is what I want you to say," she answered. "Every night we are together I think it is impossible to love you more, but now I love you a thousand times more than I did when we went to bed."

"Is that true?"

"How can I make you believe it?"

"By loving me," the Duke answered. "My darling, if only you knew how much it means to me, and how much I want your love."

"As I want yours," Janeta whispered. "Love me, Hugo . . . please . . . please love me. I am yours . . . and I want to be certain . . . that you . . . are mine."

"I will make you sure," the Duke answered.

Then he was kissing her demandingly, passionately, fiercely, and he knew as he did so he had won his crusade—he had killed the Dragon and now the Princess was his for all time.

He could feel her heart beating against him, and he knew that the fire leaping unrestrainedly within himself had kindled a flame in her.

This was love—the love he had so nearly lost—the love which God had given them and which had saved them from the evil that had threatened them.

"I love you! I love you!" Janeta was saying, and the Duke could hear the rapture in her voice.

There was no need for words.

As he made Janeta his, not only with their bodies, but with their hearts and their souls, they were joined together by the Mercy of God for all Eternity.

Barbara Cartland, the world's most famous romantic novelist, who is also an historian, playwright, lecturer, political speaker and television personality, has now written over 420 books and sold over 400 million books the world over.

She has also had many historical works published and has written four autobiographies as well as the biographies of her mother and that of her brother, Ronald Cartland, who was the first Member of Parliament to be killed in the last war. This book has a preface by Sir Winston Churchill and has just been republished with an introduction by Sir Arthur Bryant.

Love at the Helm, a novel written with the help and inspiration of the late Admiral of the Fleet, the Earl Mountbatten of Burma, is being sold for the Mountbatten Memorial Trust.

Miss Cartland in 1978 sang an Album of Love Songs with the Royal Philharmonic Orchestra.

In 1976 by writing twenty-one books, she broke the world record and has continued for the following seven years with twenty-four, twenty, twenty-three, twenty-four, twenty-four, twenty-five, and twenty-three. She is in the *Guinness Book of Records* as the best-selling author in the world.

She is unique in that she was one and two in the

Dalton List of Best Sellers, and one week had four books in the top twenty.

In private life Barbara Cartland, who is a Dame of the Order of St. John of Jerusalem, Chairman of the St. John Council in Hertfordshire and Deputy President of the St. John Ambulance Brigade, has also fought for better conditions and salaries for Midwives and Nurses.

Barbara Cartland is deeply interested in Vitamin Therapy and is President of the British National Association for Health. Her book *The Magic of Honey* has sold throughout the world and is translated into many languages. Her designs "Decorating with Love" are being sold all over the U.S.A., and the National Home Fashions League named her in 1981, "Woman of Achievement."

In 1984 she received at Kennedy Airport America's Bishop Wright Air Industry Award for her contribution to the development of aviation; in 1931 she and two R.A.F. Officers thought of, and carried, the first aeroplane-towed glider air-mail.

Barbara Cartland's Romances (a book of cartoons) has been published in Great Britain and the U.S.A., as well as a cookery book, *The Romance of Food*, and *Getting Older, Growing Younger*. She has recently written a children's pop-up picture book, entitled *Princess to the Rescue*.

BARBARA CARTLAND

Called after her own
beloved Camfield Place,
each Camfield novel of love
by Barbara Cartland
is a thrilling, never-before published
love story by the greatest romance
writer of all time.

November '86...LISTEN TO LOVE
December '86...THE GOLDEN CAGE
January '87...LOVE CASTS OUT FEAR

H1556

H1554

H1551 H1550 H1557